When I
Was Older

When I
Was Older

GARRET FREYMANN-WEYR

Houghton Mifflin Company
Boston 2000

www.hmco.com/trade

The text of this book is set in 13-point Sabon.

Book design by Celia Chetham

Library of Congress Cataloging-in-Publication Data

Freymann-Weyr, Garret.
When I was older / Garret Freymann-Weyr.
p. cm.
Summary: A new friendship with a boy who is both attractive
and intelligent helps fifteen-year-old Sophie sort out her feelings
about her younger brother Erhard, who died three years earlier,
her self-centered older sister, and her distant father.
ISBN 0-618-05545-2
[1. Death — Fiction. 2. Brothers and sisters — Fiction. 3. Fathers
and daughters — Fiction. 4. New York (N.Y.) — Fiction.] I. Title.
PZ7.F893 Wh 2000
[Fic] — dc21

Manufactured in the United States of America
RRD 10 9 8 7 6 5 4 3 2 1

For Robin, because girls rule.
And for Jeff, because so does love.

ONE

There's a ceiling hook in my bedroom, right over my desk. It used to be over my bed, but last May I rearranged all the furniture. When this was my brother's room, the hook was for a mobile from when he was a baby. When he got too old to have a mobile, it was taken down. It was probably thrown out. Nobody would have known to save it.

I could use the hook now if I wanted. There are rope holders designed for heavy plant pots. I could have a spider plant or a thatch of clover. I could even put another mobile up there. They aren't just for babies. There's an artist famous for mobiles. I can't remember his name, but Daddy took us to an exhibit at the Guggenheim where we did nothing but stare at the ceiling. At the gift shop, they were selling kits to make paper replicas of the brightly colored metal mobiles we had seen, but I didn't think to ask for one.

The point of the hook is that it's empty. The way this room would be, if Mother hadn't asked me to move into it. Daddy had already moved out of the apartment. He moved out before Erhart died, actually. Daddy was *thrown* out, Freddie would say, anxious to correct me. However you want to say it, he was gone. Without the piano, the dining room was huge again. Without Daddy, I thought the whole apartment was quiet. Mother said she liked the quiet. She needed the silent kind of quiet.

Without Erhart, the apartment was empty. It was an empty kind of quiet Mother said she couldn't bear. The way she said that, I couldn't bring myself to tell her that my moving into Erhart's room wasn't going to change anything. But, I knew Freddie was anxious to have her own room. I took up too much closet space with my old sweaters and faded skirts, which she considered to be well past their lifespan. Not to mention that she was always tripping on some pile of books or papers I had stacked neatly on the floor.

Before I moved into Erhart's room, Mother, Freddie, and I went through all of my brother's things. Mother had invited Daddy to come help, but he was too busy. She told us to take whatever we wanted and we packed up the rest for charity. For the past two years, I have had a box of my brother's things sitting under my desk. I used to have a picture of him hanging up, but I took it down when I rearranged the furniture.

I hide the picture because it gets on my nerves that the picture stays the same no matter how much I change. The trick part of remembering Erhart is that I'm different from how I was when he died. I'm fifteen now and have been for two weeks. I was twelve when my brother died. He died five days before his eighth birthday. I was in seventh grade. This year, I'm in tenth grade.

My brother stays the same, but time changes me. At the funeral and then for weeks afterwards, people told us time would heal everything. Even Daddy told me that. Actually what he said was, "Time will take care of everything, Sophie."

Everybody else said time would heal. I started saying, "Little late for healing, don't you think?" You could tell that upset people, but they got the point. They shut up. Around me, at least. Here's what time has done so far: Boys I used to be friends with call me up for dates instead. I have to wear a bra with a wire in it (and yes, I do know these two things are related). I no longer want to become a zookeeper, but a doctor who specializes in pediatric research. There's more, but thinking about what time has done to me doesn't help me remember Erhart.

Like everything else worthwhile — excellent swim times, good grades, or making Mother laugh — remembering Erhart takes practice and discipline. I think about Erhart twice every day and only on purpose. I make a special effort to not think about him by accident. That kind of sloppiness is disrespectful. I know which topics will immediately lead to him and so I steer clear of those unless it's during one of the on-purpose times.

One of the reasons I moved my bed and desk is that now I don't see the ceiling hook every time I lie down. This way, I have better control over when I do my on-purpose memories. The reason I only do them twice a day is awful, but simple: I don't have that many memories which are mine. Since I was only ten when he got sick, I didn't grasp right away that I needed to start memorizing him. A lot of what I do remember are stories that have been told to me. Instead of stories that I have told. Like the time he bit into Mother's champagne glass instead of taking a sip from it, or how he once called Daddy "Daddy Bye-Bye" because Daddy travels so much for work.

I have lots of images, but they aren't the same as memories. They show up no matter what on-purpose memory I pick. Today is Wednesday, so I can choose Erhart's seventh birthday. Because it's my favorite memory, I save it for Wednesday afternoons, Sunday mornings, and holidays. I'm in the middle of three geometry proofs involving ninety-degree angles, but on-purpose memories are more important than homework. Even math homework.

I put my pencil down and close my eyes. I let the images show up. They're never good ones, of course. They're the IVs in his arms, the white stockings the nurses wore, and the thick yellow paper inside his chart. I fold my arms, waiting for those pictures to hurry. Okay, here we are, Erhart's seventh birthday.

I take a deep breath and feel how much it is my favorite all the way into my elbows and the backs of my knees. Mother and Daddy asked him what he wanted, and since he was home unexpectedly from the hospital, there wasn't much he could have asked for that they would have said no to.

"A day out with my twin," he said, using his name for me, which was like a joke because, of course, we weren't twins.

We looked alike. This is the hardest part to remember and the most important. Photographs don't show it anymore and, besides, there aren't that many pictures. We weren't camera crazy and who knew that instead of going to concert after concert or dragging down the endless hallways of museums, we should have stayed at home documenting that we existed. Pictures or no, we did think we were twins, with Erhart accidentally born a few years after me.

I miss having a twin. The birthday outing itself — we went to see the rerelease of *Dumbo* at one of those theaters on Third Avenue behind Bloomingdales and then ate hot fudge sundaes at Serendipity — was nothing compared to his wanting to be with me. I loved how he thought we were so alike.

That's why I don't hang anything from the ceiling hook. The emptiness in the apartment that Mother wanted to fix by having me move into Erhart's room is still here. Maybe no one can see it as easily as I do, but I can feel it. And on those awful days when I can't, on those days when I can barely remember what Erhart looked like and I know that the picture I took down will make everything worse, I look at the ceiling hook. Then I can feel how empty it is without a twin. And once I can feel just how empty, I can remember everything.

TWO

Mother's met someone. A man. This is, according to my sister, a *huge* deal. He's coming to dinner tonight. An even *huger* deal, Freddie says.

"Do you realize that Mother's not been out since Erhart?" Freddie tells me.

We never say "died" to each other. We know what we mean when we use Erhart's name after the word "since."

"She has so been out. She has a job, you know."

I am folding linen napkins into triangles while Freddie wipes dust from the gilded place mats Mother asked us to put out.

"I mean out on a date," Freddie says.

"Oh, a date," I say. "That's such a *huge* deal."

Freddie and I have very different ideas about dating. Or rather, she has ideas about it and I don't. For as long as I can remember Freddie has had either a boyfriend or a crush on a boy. She really likes boys and loves dating. Up until last year, I always had boys for friends. Then one by one they started to ask me out. The thing of it was that the girls in my class who date boys do hardly anything else. Girls who I used to think were just boring I now think stupid beyond belief. I call them A-girls and it is not a compliment.

"For normal people, not going on a date for over two years *is* a huge deal," Freddie says, snatching the napkins out of my hands.

It's possible that being normal is overrated. I wasted a lot of time last year, trying to find a way to tell boys "Thanks for calling, but the minute we start dating I'm sure to bore you to death." It never came out right, though, so I always wound up saying I had a ton of homework and less time to do it in because of swim practice. After a while, they stopped calling. I have fewer friends this year and no dates.

I move the salad forks from the right of the dinner forks to the left. Freddie always gets that wrong. I barely remember all the rules about forks and glasses because we haven't set the table for company since Erhart. I remember when we used to have a lot of parties. Dinners for twelve on weeknights and open house on New Year's Day. It seemed to me that company was about fur coats and cold-earring kisses at the front door or pumpkin stew and chocolate mousse served in espresso cups at the table. It was not about dating.

I look at the table and am pleased that everything still shines and glitters. Everything still promises a happy time. At the last place setting, I move the fork and stop.

"Why did you set the table for five?" I ask Freddie.

"He's bringing his son."

"He has a son?"

"Earth to Sophie," Freddie says, which sounds mean, but she is laughing. "Yes, he has a son. Do you listen to anything anyone says outside of a classroom?"

"Sometimes," I say, going over what I know about Mother's date.

His name is Nick Roberts and we met him last week when he came to pick Mother up for a movie. He's fourteen years older than Mother, but he doesn't look old so much as tired. His face is really thin, but his features are big. Freddie says he's funny looking, but I think he's handsome. Not the way Daddy is, but in his own way. Nick teaches history and writes books and his last book won a big prize, so City College offered him a job, which started in September.

I remember about the son now. He's the reason behind each of Nick's new jobs. Five years ago, Nick left his job at Portland University in Oregon and started teaching at a prep school in Massachusetts. It was a few years after his wife died, Mother said, and he wanted to spend more time with his son and less time dealing with the hassles of a history department. Nick took the job he has now at City College because he thought his son needed to experience life outside of small-town New England.

There's only one explanation for how I could have forgotten all this: the minute anybody mentions death, my brain clicks right off. This is an extremely bad habit which I thought I had under control.

"Why is Nick bringing his son?"

"Maybe he couldn't find a baby-sitter," Freddie says, shrugging.

"I thought he was our age," I say.

"Your age, maybe. Too young for me."

Freddie won't turn eighteen until February, but she is dating a graduate student and is very fixated on how grown-up she is. They met when she was waiting for Daddy at Lincoln Center. Daddy never showed, but for once Freddie didn't care. *A graduate student.* She must think that to herself a million times a day.

We hear Mother calling and head to the

kitchen. She looks really pretty, but her hands are all covered with tomatoes and basil.

"Girls, they'll be here in about five minutes," she says, trying to push her hair back without getting gunk in it. "Let's be in the living room and all relaxed when they arrive."

Freddie gives Mother some damp paper towels to wipe her hands with.

"I thought you couldn't relax," I say.

"She can't," Freddie says. "We have to help her pretend."

"Pretend really well," Mother says. "Nick says he feels totally relaxed in my company."

She giggles. An honest to God A-girl giggle. The doorbell rings and we all freeze.

"It'll be fine," Freddie says. "Everything will be fine."

She gives Mother a hug.

"It will, won't it?' Mother asks me anxiously.

I don't say anything. I mean, what does "fine" mean, anyway? After all, even Daddy is "fine."

Freddie gives me a little shove.

"Let's go, sunshine," she says, and then in a low whisper adds, *"They're here."*

I know she's imitating the little girl from *Poltergeist* in order to make me smile. But I also know that the actress who played the girl died in a hospital when she was only twelve. So I don't smile. I just follow her out of the room and toward the company.

THREE

Mother and Nick kiss hello. On the cheek, more friendly than anything else, but still. Nick introduces his son to us and I immediately forget his name. There's this thing on his face which at first I think is a scar. Only it's too perfect-looking to be a scar. It's a tattoo! A tattoo in the shape of a teardrop, about an inch below the outer edge of his left eye. I am dying to stare at it and decide if I think it's a smart or a stupid thing. Instead, I turn away quickly and ask Nick for his coat.

"Here you go, Sophie," Nick says with a smile that's shy and a little nervous, but sweet.

I feel bad about not remembering his son's name. I wonder what Nick said when he saw the tattoo for the first time. I try to imagine Daddy's expression if I did that to my face. Not a pretty picture, believe me. I take Nick's coat and head into Mother's bedroom, where I see that Freddie has already dumped the son's coat on the bed.

Back in the living room, I put ice in glasses for Freddie's bitter lemon and Nick's brandy and soda. Mother's drinking a glass of wine, which is nice to see since she and Daddy used to have wine-hour before dinner every night. Nick's son shakes his head no. Doesn't want anything. I stay leaning against the bar.

The son is sitting on the edge of the dark green chaise longue. He looks a lot like Nick but completely different at the same time. He's very tall and his whole body is like a collection of bones, wrists, and knees. His face is thin like Nick's, but his features fit it. The tattoo, while definitely eye-catching, doesn't seem out of place. He keeps moving around like he's trying to fit ten-mile-long arms and legs into a two-mile place. *He's cute,* part of me thinks. I wonder if noticing his being cute is the same thing as having a crush on him. I doubt it. Puppies are cute too, and no one dates them.

I stop looking so he won't think I'm staring at the tattoo. Which I am. I try to catch Freddie's eye to see what she thinks of someone who has a tear engraved on his face, but she is on the far end of the sofa, looking out of the window at Central Park instead of at Nick, who is sitting between her and Mother.

"Sophie has one," Mother says in response

to something Nick says. "But I don't think she uses it so much."

Uses what?

Without even having to turn around, Freddie knows I've spaced out and she clues me in by saying to Mother, "That's because you won't let her have a modem."

My computer. Why are we talking about my computer?

"That's not why I don't use it. I don't want to go on-line. You're the one who wants to use e-mail."

"You can do a lot more on-line than e-mail," Nick's son says. "You can look things up and talk to people in other countries. You can make reservations and find out stuff you didn't even know you wanted to know."

"Francis had computer access at Meadow-brooke Academy and he really misses it," Nick says to Mother.

Francis, that's right. He has a girl's name, my sister has a boy's name, and I have three: Anna Sophia Maria. No wonder I can never remember anybody's name. I look at Francis now, not staring, but curious about what he's thinking behind that tattoo.

"You can also go to the library and find out stuff," I say. "I hardly have time to talk to anybody here, let alone in other countries."

"What makes you so busy?" he asks, as if I have a problem I need help with.

"Homework," I say.

Freddie leans forward. Slender and blonde, she fixes her gaze on Francis and says, "Sophie is very smart."

Which happens to be true enough, but when said like that by your beautiful older sister to a cute boy with a tattoo, it means, *Sophie is dull and sort of a geek. Which explains the way she looks, in case you were wondering.*

"And swim practice," I add hastily. "I don't get home until five-thirty or so. Anyway, I think people who choose to spend their free time zoned into a computer screen, convinced that they're really *talking* just because they're typing, are crazy."

He runs one of his hands over the top of his head and right before his hair falls back into his face, the tattoo flashes at me. With his hair falling forward, you can still see it, but it's not as stark.

"And then, of course, there are the people who really have something to communicate," he says. "Like the students at Tiananmen who got a lot of the truth out to the world by fax and e-mail before the tanks rolled. The Internet has the capacity to let truth triumph no matter what

16

kind of oppressive censorship is in place."

I don't have anything to say to that. Tiananmen is a square someplace in China where a lot of people were killed. I could be wrong. All those people died in China when I was ten.

"We followed Tiananmen with a lot of fervor at Meadowbrooke Academy," Nick says. "It was Francis's introduction to the world."

Meadowbrooke Academy is the school in Meadowbrooke, Massachusetts, where Nick and Francis moved to from Oregon. After Nick's wife died, I remind myself sternly. It doesn't seem fair to wonder about Francis's tattoo but let my brain click off when it comes to his mother dying. I am always insulted when people act as if Erhart's dying means he was never alive.

"I was already introduced to the world. Massachusetts *is* part of the world," Francis says to his father. "New York's not the center of the universe, you know."

"It's not?" Nick asks with mock surprise. "Then what are we doing here?"

"Expanding my horizons," Francis says, in a very funny imitation of his father's voice. "Which would be a lot easier with a computer of my own!"

Suddenly I like him without worrying if I have a crush. He fidgets a lot, but his brain obviously works, and for all I know, he's smarter than I am.

"I'm giving it some thought," Nick says, his shy, sweet smile spreading across his face once again. "If only to save on phone bills."

"Phone bills?" Mother asks.

"Most of my friends are still at Meadowbrooke," Francis says. "I'm on the phone a lot."

The fact that making new friends would be cheaper than buying a computer lodges itself in my brain, and I have to fight not to let it out of my mouth.

"Sophie, we have a few minutes before dinner is ready," Mother says. "Take Francis and show him yours."

Oh, sure. She knows I can never talk to people I don't know. I'll probably wind up insulting him. I do that often and easily. It's not that I don't think; it's that I do. And when I'm thinking, I usually forget about what not to say.

I push myself away from the bar. "Okay."

Francis untangles himself from the chaise longue.

"It's nothing that great," I say as we round the corner from the living room, through the front hall, and into the small hallway where our own coats hang.

"A hallway off a hallway," Francis says.

"This place is huge."

We go in the bedroom and I see the bedsheets are rumpled and that my books are not as neatly arranged as they would have been if I'd known company was not only coming to dinner, but into my room. He does not focus on the mess, but the space.

"Wow. Pretty big."

It is a big apartment, although I never thought that until after Daddy and his piano moved out.

"It is kind of big," I say.

"This place is huge compared to where Nick and I live," Francis says.

He calls his father Nick? I wonder if I would call Daddy by his first name if Mother died. The idea that Mother might die and leave us with Daddy reminds me why my brain clicks off when the topic of death comes up. It always leads to something awful. I point at my desk.

"That's it," I say.

"A Mac," Francis says. "Cool."

"The idea is, or was, that when I go to medical school, it'll be upgraded."

"You're going to medical school?" Francis asks while trying to fold himself into the ergonomically correct desk chair I inherited from Mother.

He's got his feet where his knees should be,

which defeats the chair's whole purpose; to make you sit up straight. It's how I sit in it too. I love slouching.

"Well, not right away," I answer, trying to make eye contact without staring. "After college."

I can't believe it's a tear. Why not a flower?

"What's that?" he asks. "In like six years?"

And it's green. A green tear. I suppose a tattoo can't really be clear-colored. I nod. Yes, six years. "So?"

"How do you know what you're going to want to be in six years?"

"If I wait until then to decide, it will be too late," I point out.

Maybe he's not as smart as I thought. Hello, MCATs anyone? Not to mention getting through my premed requirements.

"It'll also be too late to change your mind," he says.

"I'm not going to," I say.

Henry Silver, my one best friend at school, has a black belt in karate and almost all the men in his class have tattoos, but on their arms and backs. Not on their faces.

Francis puts his feet on the floor and wheels the chair toward me. Before I realize what he's doing, he's grabbed my hand and pressed it against his face, over the tattoo. I'm so surprised, I don't even think to jerk back, although the truth is I don't like to be this close to people.

"It's just skin," he says, rubbing my fingertips back and forth over the tear.

"Why is it on your face?" I ask, pleased that I don't sound as scared as I feel. Coping with other people is not what I'm best at. It makes me nervous, anxious, and terrified.

"For people to see."

His voice is calm and he takes his hand away from mine, so that if I wanted to, I could move my fingers away. Which I do. I wonder if he could tell that my hand was shaking.

"You can ask me anything you want about it," he says. "But stop staring at me as if you aren't."

Up this close, I can see that his eyes are green. Not the dark, muddy green of the tattoo, but bright and clear. My hand is still shaking and I can't decide if my fingers are nervous from excitement or horror. He is cute, and touching his tattoo was touching him. Which maybe I wanted to do. I hope I didn't. Did he want me to touch him? Do I want him to want me to? Could I sound more boring?

"I'm sorry," I say, finally. "I was trying not to."

"Just stop trying."

"I'll try," I say, and we both laugh.

FOUR

Ever since Daddy moved out, we've eaten at the round white table in the kitchen. It's impossible to sit in the dining room and not miss how everything used to be. Whenever company came, Mother and Daddy rented tables and chairs for the front hall, and with candles lit, the bookshelves cast elegant shadows and you could see the piano through the dining room's glass doors.

I am seated across the table from Nick and next to Francis. We could all, I suppose, pass for normal. Nick looks less tired and — Mother was right — he seems relaxed in her company. Mother has made a really good pasta dish with three different kinds of mushrooms and some eggplant thrown in for good measure. Freddie, who is a chronic dieter, makes a big show of eating only about three bites before asking for the salad. She doesn't exactly exert herself to keep the conversation going. A peaceful silence settles over the table until Francis asks for a second helping.

"This is probably the best dinner Nick has eaten since I took over the kitchen," Francis tells Mother, passing his plate down.

"You call your father 'Nick'?" Freddie asks him.

She sounds like she is accusing him of murder.

"Yeah," Francis answers. "It's his name."

"That doesn't bother you?" Freddie asks, turning toward Nick.

"It did at first," Nick says. "But it was Francis's preference. I got used to it."

"Your father tells me you're a wonderful cook," Mother says, and I can tell that if she weren't too far away, she'd give Freddie a little kick under the table. A little kick that said *Drop it.*

"I do all right," Francis says.

"How come you took over the kitchen?" I ask.

The only thing I can make in the kitchen is a plate of Oreos. Freddie, who is very good in the kitchen, couldn't care less about why Francis cooks for his father. She looks across the table at Francis and fires her question at him before he can answer mine.

"Why do you call your father by his first name?" she asks.

"Freddie, that's enough," Mother says softly, but with metal sparks flying out of her voice.

Francis holds up his hand and smiles at Mother. "No, it's okay, Mrs. Merdinger," he says.

He looks back at Freddie. "When my mother died, calling Nick 'Dad' constantly reminded me that there was no one to call 'Mom.' So I started using his first name and I've just never stopped."

"Oh," Freddie says. "That makes a lot of sense."

She looks back down at her plate and starts eating her salad again. I can tell she's mortified that she's forced Francis to talk about *his* dead mother on *our* mother's date.

Francis turns to me. "I took over the kitchen because I was tired of eating steak and potatoes."

"I can cook more than that," Nick says by way of a protest.

"That's true," Francis says. "There was the lamb chops and rice."

"I made salad," Nick says to Mother. "Really, he makes it sound just terrible."

"Your idea of salad is a head of lettuce with French dressing," Francis says.

"My father is a good cook," Freddie says.

Only for other women. I manage to think this without saying it. A major accomplishment.

"That's good," Francis says. "Men should know how to cook. There's every likelihood that they'll wind up alone."

There's just enough sarcasm in his voice for me to think that he knows Daddy lives alone and why.

There's a very still silence in the room that's not at all like the peaceful kind from earlier. I realize that nobody is going to say anything. It's as if my father has actually shown up. What to say? It's a well-known family fact that I get my terror of social talk from Mother. Freddie gets her ease and grace from Daddy, but she only uses it for her own convenience.

"What's it like living here after so long in Massachusetts?" I ask, finally coming up with something to say.

"The neighborhood took a little getting used to," Nick says.

"Where do you live?" I ask, wishing my legs were long enough to reach Freddie's foot under the table. Getting a group conversation going only works if more than one person is involved.

"On Eighty-first Street between Lexington and Third Avenue," Nick says.

"That's very posh," I say.

"The apartment is rent-controlled," Nick says. "It belongs to a friend of mine at Meadowbrooke Academy. He hasn't lived here in years, but just never let go of it."

"What took getting used to?" I ask Nick.

I love that neighborhood. Everything is hushed and elegant. They practically have chandeliers instead of street lamps.

"It's a little sterile," Nick says. "Francis has never really lived in a city and I think it's hard to judge city life based on the Upper East Side."

"Jeez, Nick, I do leave the area, you know."

"You don't like it?" I ask Francis, incredulous.

I would do a lot to live in a rent-controlled apartment on the Upper East Side.

"No, I don't like it," Francis says.

"Why not?"

"Well, how many stores selling eight-dollar jam does a neighborhood need? We must have like ten a block."

"Three is more like it," Nick says, but I can tell that he basically agrees with Francis.

"Those stores are nice," I say. "They have teas that smell like vanilla and cookies made in Belgium."

I know I sound ridiculous talking about tea and cookies as if I were eleven. A dumb eleven.

"Yeah, I know," Francis says in an almost

sarcastic way. "But other than spending money, what can you do there?"

"Go to a museum or a doctor," Freddie says, and I wonder what exactly is bugging her. She's always loved walking around the East Side with me.

"Both of which involve spending money," Francis says. "Going to the Metropolitan costs seven-fifty."

Freddie rolls her eyes. "That's only the suggested admission. Nobody *pays* that."

"How civic-minded of you," Francis says, totally sarcastic this time, no almost about it.

"The Frick is free for students on Thursday afternoons," I say.

I know this because I'm on their mailing list, which doesn't cost anything, and their newsletter had an item about a government grant for educational viewing. Otherwise it's eight dollars to get in and they don't have a student rate.

"Is that the mansion down near Seventieth? On Fifth Avenue?" Francis asks.

"Yes," I say. "It's great. I wish I lived there."

"How did it become a museum?" Francis asks.

Nick sighs. "How is it that my son has never heard of Henry Clay Frick?"

"I know who he is," Francis says. "Turn-of-the-century industrialist. Made all his money in coal and steel. I just didn't know he owned a museum."

"When Frick owned it, it was his private house," Nick says. "Now it's a public museum."

"Public for people with money to spare," Francis says.

"Sophie, why don't you take Francis to the Frick tomorrow, if it's free," Mother says oh-so-sweetly. "Then you can walk down to Serendipity and show him another neighborhood plus. You used to go there with Erhart all the time."

My protests of having swim practice and being behind in my homework choke each other. I hate when she does that. She says it's normal and healthy to weave Erhart into conversation, but I am never prepared for it.

"That's a great idea," Nick says. "Francis, what time's your tutoring over tomorrow?"

"Two," Francis says to him. To me, "You want to? I'd like to see the inside of this mansion-museum thing."

"Sure, but, I, you know, I have practice."

"So you'll go to practice in the morning," Mother says. "Coffee?" she asks Nick, who nods his head yes.

"There is ice cream and blueberries for dessert," Mother says, standing up. She motions

Nick. "This is the part of the meal that I never have to serve."

They head across the hallway to the living room. Freddie pushes her plate in my direction.

"I'll do dessert," she says. "You clear."

Francis puts Freddie's plate on top of his and then those on top of mine.

"I'll help," he says.

I take the plates away from him. "No, you'd better go with them. You're company and company doesn't help."

"What is that, a rule?"

"Yes, actually, it is."

He folds his hands under his arms and then stuffs them into his pants pockets.

"So, should we meet out in front of the Frick or inside?"

"I guess in front's okay," I say, not wanting to wander around looking for him or to get found while I'm looking at something I like a lot. I think that things you like are private.

"Okay. What time?"

What time, what time? I have an essay outline due in English tomorrow. I have a set of physics problems due on Friday and an Italian test on Monday. What time? No time, never, thank you.

"My last period ends at 3:05, so, I don't know, 3:30?"

"Okay."

Francis's hand makes its way back from his pocket to under his arm. He then touches my face, rubbing a spot right under my left eye.

"Right there," he says. "Yours would be right there."

Although I feel less afraid than I first did in my bedroom, I would rather he had dragged my hand across *his* face again instead of touching *mine*. I feel full of curiosity about him, but I don't want people to be curious about me. I know I would want a boyfriend if I could figure out how to have one without turning into an A-girl. I can't explain any of this to him so I just step back a little.

"I'll see you tomorrow," I say.

"Okay," he says, walking past me to the doorway. "Tomorrow."

I carry the plates out to the pantry door toward my sister. Toward dessert.

FIVE

They stay until almost nine-thirty, which means I have exactly forty-five minutes before bedtime in which to do my homework. There are some geometry proofs I can finish during history class, and vocabulary words for Italian which I already memorized. Physics I can do tomorrow night. My real problem is English. I'm good at grammar and always finish my reading assignments. However, I'm *not* good at essay questions based on what I've read. And I'm terrible at the kind of essay question Mr. Gallagher has assigned as a semester project.

Last week, he asked everyone to write down and turn in a paragraph about the one thing in the world they most disliked. I wrote down *I dislike time because it passes.* The next day he told us that we had to write a free-form essay which explores the nature of what we dislike. Mr. Gallagher said that if we can't express clearly what we dislike, we will have no idea who we are as people. The whole point of reading and writing, he told us, is to discover who we are.

The outline is due tomorrow. I have one sentence so far. "The dictionary defines time as 'a continuous measurable quantity in which events occur in an irreversible sequence.'" I open the thesaurus Daddy left behind with his dictionary. "Some other words for time include *duration, period, term, stage, span, spell,* and *season.*"

I read over my two pathetic sentences. Ought to put me right into the top ten percent of my class. I worry a lot about getting into medical school and think it would be a fine joke for someone if I never get in because of my tenth-grade English class.

I lie down on my bed and wonder how I can possibly write an entire essay on time without once mentioning that my brother died.

Freddie pokes her head in through the door that connects her room to mine. "I can see you're studying hard," she says.

I sit up. "I was resting my brain."

"Well, that always gets my homework done."

"Sarcasm does not become you," I say, which is something she and Mother tell me all the time.

Freddie curls up on the wooden covered radiator that's next to my bed and under the window. She wraps the shade's cord around her fingers.

"So," she says.

I put my stuffed bear from a thousand years ago behind me as if it were a bolster.

"So," I say back.

It's been a long time since Freddie came in for a powwow. I was sure she would the night Daddy moved out. When she didn't, I thought about going into her room, but I was afraid I might cry. It turned out that we were both saving our tears for when Erhart died. We both cried a lot then.

"You like him." She says this more than asks it and I think, God, was I that obvious? I'm not even sure I do like him. *Like-like* as opposed to just like.

I shrug.

"Mother does," Freddie says, and I realize that she is talking about Nick.

I think about the glass of wine Mother had before dinner. The way she laughed at Nick's teaching stories. The way he caught her eye to smile right at her.

"Yes," I say. "She does."

"He's kind of odd," Freddie says. "He's spent his whole life in school either teaching or studying."

"He's a teacher," I say. "A professor, really."

"Francis is even stranger," she says.

"He's not bad," I say.

"They are so the opposite of Daddy," she says, tucking her knees up under her chin.

I don't say anything. Freddie and I try to avoid any and all direct conversation about our father. We both love him, of course, but my sister also likes him. A lot.

"The women Daddy dates," Freddie says, and then stops. She presses her nose against the window. "They are way more like Mother than Nick is like Daddy."

"There are way more of Daddy's dates than there are of Mother's," I say without thinking. "You'd think he'd go for a little variety."

Freddie stands up and my shade snaps up around its rollers and spins wildly. She stands over the bed, staring down at me.

"Finish your homework, little genius," she says finally.

"I didn't mean it that way," I say.

"Night," Freddie says, and vanishes into her room.

There are a lot of things I'd like to ask my sister, but because we almost never see eye-to-eye about Daddy, most of our conversations end with her stomping away from me. Totally offended. It's such a drag, because I know that there are things she could help me with. Like last year, I wanted her advice about boys.

Freddie's really beautiful. Unlike an A-girl, she doesn't need to change anything about herself for the sake of her boyfriends. I thought she might have been able to help me find a way to stay friends with the boys I didn't want to date. But she was always too mad at me about Daddy for me to ever ask her about anything, let alone boys.

I know Freddie and her graduate student are having sex, because I heard her and Mother talking about it. Mother told Freddie that she had no problem with Freddie's having sex when she was so clearly in love, but to be sure and only have safe sex, et cetera. Mother also said that Ian seemed a little too old. Freddie said that Daddy didn't think so. It seems unfair that my sister will talk to my father about sex, but not to me. It's not like he needs to learn anything about it. Oh, well.

I go back to my desk and look at my two-sentence essay outline. I decide to tell Mr. Gallagher that I will be handing it in late as an exploration of the role time plays in deadlines. That should buy me at least a week — a *duration* of seven twenty-four-hour *periods*. A *season* in which to think and outline the mystery of *time*. I don't think he'll be thrilled, but it's the best I can do.

SIX

In the morning, I am the first one at the pool. Aside from Coach Alden, of course. I think she lives here. She is sitting on the diving board, which is her favorite place to observe workouts from.

"Good for you, Sophie," she says, unbearably loud and cheery. "I told you that a couple of weeks of double workouts is all you need to shave that time of yours down."

"This isn't a double workout," I say, walking along the pool's edge toward the girls' room. "I'm not coming this afternoon."

I can tell she's disappointed without even looking at her. No one else shows up except Justin Hawker, who wants to be captain next year. Justin and I were best friends all through grammar school. We did everything together, including his math homework. Whenever he got less than an A on his math assignments, he would blame me and say I was the stupidest smart girl he knew.

He meant it in a sweet way, and aside from Erhart, he was my favorite person, until he started hanging around with a bunch of boys I call the Wolf Pack. We were still friends, though, until last year. He was the boy who phoned me the most to ask about going out. We hardly talk anymore, but he's got a good pull on the crawl and I'll probably vote for him to be captain.

Coach Alden blows the whistle and we dive into our separate lanes. The trick with swimming is not to think about what you're doing. The minute you realize how boring it is — back and forth, back and forth — it's impossible not to slow down. I usually think about my homework or medical school or the cities I want to live in some day: Boston, San Francisco, Rome, or London. I won't have any choice for the first ten or fifteen years of my career, because I'll be tied to a research hospital, but it's nice to pretend.

This morning, however, I think about Francis, which is stupid, irritating, and, very quickly, boring. Maybe I won't do pediatrics research. Maybe I'll invent a chemical compound that will let you think about a boy without losing your mind.

* * *

School is its usual nightmare blend of good classes and unbearable people. I have history first and second period, which I like this term because we're doing systems of government: bicameral, parliamentary, totalitarian, military, communist, and anarchic. It's the easiest class I have and I usually sit in the back with Henry Silver so we can do geometry homework.

"You smell like the pool," he says, passing me my notes from yesterday.

Henry never takes notes. He fills his notebook up with chess diagrams and says that if he needs to know anything outside of the assigned reading, our teachers have failed him. During history, I give him all of my notes from the day before and he looks to see if there's anything in them he might need. There usually is. Henry may be a genius, a chess prodigy, and a black belt in karate, but his grades are terrible. Talent is a good thing, I like to tell him, but so is hard work.

"Chlorine's a disinfectant," I say. "You want to smell French perfume, get notes from an A-girl."

Henry rolls his eyes. He is the only boy I know who has not tried to treat me like a girl. Ever. I wonder if he notices that I am one, but I think he just likes me. I'm his only friend outside of his karate class or his chess tutor. Henry and Justin Hawker never liked each other, and the boys Justin pals around with have, according to Henry, "no focus." I may smell like a pool, but I have focus. In spades.

Third period is Italian with Mrs. Caccini, who looks younger than Freddie, wears chopsticks in her hair and has the biggest eyes you have ever seen. Someday I will go to Rome on a Fulbright grant and during breaks from my important lab research, I will sit in a *caffè*. There I will drink red wine and eat bottomless bowls of pasta while graciously fending off the ardent attentions of more admirers than can fit at my round table. I will wear gray tights over my suddenly long and skinny legs, a flouncy, short black skirt and — why not? — chopsticks in my magically long, straight, well-behaved hair.

Mrs. Caccini is very popular. I think everyone spends her class dreaming up a way to go to Italy. Henry takes Russian. He says no decent chess player has ever come out of Italy and that the only good medical care you can get in Europe is in France. I told him French was for snobs, and that shut him up.

* * *

Fourth period is geometry. We have assigned seats because Mr. Kelley says he can never put names to faces. This way he can memorize the seating chart. When he calls on you, you never know if he knows who you are or if he is simply expecting an answer from the person third on the left in the second row.

He has bushy black eyebrows and a skinny body that twitches under his thick corduroy jackets. He used to throw erasers at people who talked in class, but once, a boy he was aiming at ducked and the eraser flew smack into a girl's chest and she cried. He almost got fired and had to stop throwing them, but everyone is still always very nervous when he picks up the eraser. It makes his classes a little more exciting.

Fifth period is lunch and I realize that I forgot to bring mine. I ask Henry if he can split his sandwich with me and he gives me a whole one. He eats the same thing every day: two peanut butter and honey sandwiches, five Oreos, an apple, and three dried figs.

"Do you want my cookies too?" he asks.

"No," I say.

If I told him that last night a boy with a tattoo on his face had come to our house for dinner and that I had touched him, Henry would probably look at me as if I had grown another head. I pinch myself behind the knee to stop thinking about Francis. It's not like we have a date. We're just meeting at the Frick. I shake my head.

"What?" Henry asks.

"Nothing," I say, grateful that he can't read my mind. I pinch my knee again, but harder. "Nothing."

Henry hates English class more than I do. He says Mr. Gallagher should focus less on who we are as people and more on teaching. We both stare at the pile of paperback books on Mr. Gallagher's desk. I was wondering when we would start reading something. When Mr. Gallagher asks us to pass up our essay outlines, I fold mine in half so no one can see that it's only a paragraph long. Henry's essay is on music and his outline is three pages.

"We're going to spend the rest of the semester reading *Hamlet*," Mr. Gallagher says, and I think, Oh great.

I read the play when Freddie had to read it when she was in tenth grade and then Daddy took us to a production of it somewhere in Brooklyn. Basically, everybody dies. Hamlet spends the whole play trying to figure out if his uncle killed his father and if so, what he should do for revenge. It's endless, and there will be no way to avoid the topic of death if we have to write any essays on it.

"Cool," Henry says. "I've always loved sword fights."

"Sword fights?" I ask, and then remember that everybody dies by getting stabbed. Or taking poison. Or drowning. I think Henry read the collected works of Shakespeare when he was nine. On a dare. If he weren't so strange, I would have to hate him for being so smart.

During study hall, I reread the first act of *Hamlet*. It's much better than I had remembered. I have physics last period, and it's easy without being interesting. I take notes as a way of staying awake. On a separate sheet of paper I make a list of things to talk to Francis about: paintings, Massachusetts, and maybe Tiananmen Square. That should keep us occupied for the afternoon without straying anywhere dangerous.

SEVEN

We can't get into the Frick for free because Francis doesn't have a school ID. Nick, Francis tells me, can't afford private school and thinks that the New York City public school system is atrocious. Between us, we have six dollars and one ID. Not enough to get us inside the Frick.

"How are you going to get into college?" I ask him, after it has been established that neither of us has any idea of what to do with the afternoon.

"Apply," he says, and I am no longer full of curiosity about him; he is a jerk.

"You mean because I'm not in high school?" Francis asks as it finally dawns on him that I don't think "apply" is an answer.

I am suddenly so nervous I think I might throw up. We can't go to the museum, so he must want to go home. Here I am wasting his time asking stupid questions about college. And mine, I'm wasting my time too. Why I am so nervous about a boy who is an obvious jerk?

"I get tutored," Francis says. "Nick has a friend who preps people for the bar exam. He gives me lessons."

Now I get to be a jerk back.

"You want to take the bar, huh? How do you know you're going to want to do that in six years?"

"No, not the bar, high school stuff," Francis says, trailing off as he remembers our conversation last night. "Right. Funny. Anyway, it's five years. I'm considerably older than you."

"Oh, sure. What are you, a whopping sixteen?"

"Just turned seventeen," he says. "Not even two weeks ago. September twelfth."

September twelfth is *my* birthday, and I tell him so. He's rocking back on his heels and also doing that irritating thing with his hands where he moves them from under his arms into his pockets. Arms/pockets, arms/pockets. It's driving me crazy. That and wondering how much he's dying to go home and if I should do my essay outline for Mr. Gallagher tonight or wait a week as I had planned.

"I wonder if that makes us twins," Francis

says, and I feel everything go dangerously still. "You know, born apart by a couple of years through an accident of time."

Not to mention born apart by a couple of mothers, one of whom is now dead. Go on, Sophie, say it. What I do instead solves the problem of how Francis and I are going to spend the afternoon: I cry and he gives me things.

As he scrounges around in his pockets for a Kleenex, he says, "You don't even have to get a tattoo. That's the great part of being separated twins."

Now I'm embarrassed, as well as cold, tired, and sick to my stomach. For the past couple of years, I've wanted to throw up every time I get upset. I haven't done it yet, but feeling like I'm going to is unpleasant enough.

It's not just that Francis has made me think about Erhart by accident, it's that I haven't thought of him at all today. I promised him that he would always live in my memory, but I was in such a hurry this morning because of swim practice and then busy all day. The worst part is that I could have made time during study hall, but I didn't even think about it.

"I'm sorry," I say, right before blowing my nose. "I don't always get like this."

Francis looks closely at me before asking, "Like what?"

"Cold and weepy," I say. "And about to throw up."

"Ah, jeez," he says, shrugging off his jacket and swinging it around my shoulders. "Let's walk. It'll get your blood moving and I'll buy you a pretzel at the corner."

"A pretzel?"

"It's bread," Francis says. "Get some bread in your stomach and you'll feel better."

"There's no scientific basis for that," I say, although a pretzel does sound good.

"Maybe not, but I make Nick toast whenever he's got the flu," Francis says. "Toast and drunken tea."

Daddy used to make me drunken tea when he still lived with us. If I was incredibly nervous before an exam and I couldn't sleep, Daddy would put equal parts sugar and whisky into some lemon tea and sit with me while I drank it down. Now if I can't sleep, I have to count backwards from one hundred.

Francis buys the pretzel for me at a hot dog stand. The man, who's short and thick bodied and wearing two flannel shirts and an old pair of pants, takes the $1.75 Francis gives him.

"There's something on your face, son," he says.

"It's a tear," Francis says, taking some extra napkins from the little metal canister, which is balanced on top of the soda display.

"I can see that," the hot dog man says. "What's it doing on your face?"

"It's kind of private," Francis says.

"If it's so private, why is it on your face?" the hot dog man asks, handing Francis a huge, salt-encrusted pretzel.

"So I can see it," Francis says.

Last night he said it was on his face *for people to see*. Maybe I'm not remembering correctly.

"Have a good day," Francis says, sounding so pleasant that the man actually smiles at him.

We cross Fifth Avenue and walk uptown toward the Metropolitan Museum, which we could go into for a dollar each except that he doesn't think it's very civic-minded. I notice that he's not eating any of the pretzel he's gone to such great lengths to buy. Or giving it to me, which is just as well. If I even try and swallow I will throw up all over him. I take a deep, slow breath.

"Do you want to go home?" I ask. "I mean, our plans are not happening as they should so you don't have to . . ."

Francis stops walking.

"I'm having a good time," he says. "If you want to go home, go ahead."

"No, I mean, I do have stuff to do, but this is fine."

"What exactly is this stuff that you have to do other than burst into tears?"

I know I'm furious, but I'm not sure what to say and, inexplicably, instead of telling him about how my essay outline is late, I say something true.

"I cried because you reminded me of something I haven't done yet. Something I have to do."

"What?" Francis asks.

"It's none of your business," I say.

"Ah, don't be that way. I've made you mad and I don't know why. Just explain what you mean. Please?"

It really is none of his business, but a little polite asking goes a long way with me and so I try to explain. About on-purpose remembering. About how little there is to remember and yet how much. About how Erhart wouldn't even know me now.

"Do you want to have an on-purpose time now?" Francis asks.

"Here?"

"We could sit on that bench."

"I don't feel well," I say, hoping that I will quickly overcome this truth-telling jag I'm on.

"You just need to eat," Francis says, taking my hands and wrapping them around the pretzel.

We sit on the bench and he watches as I take a bite. The pretzel is still warm and the act of chewing calms me down immediately.

"When you're done eating, we can do an on-purpose remember."

"No," I say. "It's a private just-for-me kind of thing. Private like why you have a tear on your face."

"It's only private sometimes," he says, stuffing his hands into his pockets.

Here we go again, I think, but his hands stay put as Francis surveys the soaring and multi-windowed apartment buildings across the street.

"My mother died when I was eight," Francis says, his eyes fixed firmly across the street. "Right before my eighth birthday, actually."

My brain freezes. Literally. I quietly spit the pretzel I'm chewing into my hand and drop it behind the bench. Erhart died right before his eighth birthday. I look at Francis and try to remember what my brother looked like. He looked like me. Not like this tall, strange boy.

"At some point it occurred to me that the number of years she had been dead would be longer than the number of years I had known her."

50

This is math. My brain thaws. Francis knew his mother for eight years. His mother has now been dead for nine years. One year longer than he knew her.

I turn the math on myself. I knew Erhart for eight years. When I turn twenty-one, I will have spent one more year without my brother than with him.

"So I decided to bring her with me wherever I went," Francis says, moving his eyes from the buildings to me.

He points at the tattoo.

"Crying, watching Nick cry, being told not to cry. It was the best thing I could think of."

"When did you get it done?" I ask.

"I was thirteen. It was stupid."

"I don't think it's stupid," I say, and I don't, although it does make it impossible for him to have any privacy about his mother's death.

"If I had been smart," Francis says, "I would have thought of doing on-purpose memories."

"I didn't want to waste them," I say.

"Yeah. I think I have about three of my mother. Maybe five. It was really smart of you, Sophie."

"It's just different," I say. "I like the tattoo. It's very concrete."

"It made Nick feel bad," Francis says. "He thought he had done something wrong that I should take such a . . . what did he say? Such a drastic action."

I like the sound those words make. *Such a drastic action.* It's hard to picture Nick getting too upset at anything. And the tattoo is still there. He didn't march Francis to a doctor's office for laser surgery or anything. I look at Francis's face and try to picture it without the tear. I put the hand not holding my pretzel over the tattoo and smile at him.

"It *is* just skin," I say, amazed at how calm I feel.

It's still impossible to tell what he would look like without the tear. As I pull my hand away, Francis catches it between both of his.

"Your fingers are freezing," he says.

I look down at our hands. He has laced our fingers together so that we have gone from talking to holding hands. I am sitting on Fifth Avenue holding hands with a boy. I try to have an interesting thought to see if I am still myself. I can't come up with even one word of Italian. Whatever physics I once knew is on vacation. I try to picture a right triangle, but can only see a square.

Francis slowly puts one of his hands on my face and leans gently toward me.

"I've never kissed anybody," I say quickly,

pulling my head as far back as I can without moving my body.

"I've never kissed anybody who hasn't," he says. "So we're even."

"No," I say, releasing my hand from his and moving his other hand away from my face. "You kiss me and it's no big deal to you. I kiss you and it's my first time."

"It's only your first time once," he says. "We can kiss twice."

He's not exactly agreeing with me, but he moves just far enough away so that I can calm down a bit without having to panic that he's going to walk off forever with no chance for me to explain. Maybe Francis will turn out to be like Justin Hawker, but so far he's just strange for a guy. Without being strange in the way Henry is.

"The first time you kissed a girl, were you different after?" I ask him, staring at my hands, which are now hopelessly tangled up in my lap.

"Well, yeah," he says.

"How?"

"Before I kissed her I was insanely nervous. See your hands? My whole body was in more knots than that. So, after, I was relieved. And I wanted to do it again. Right away."

"It's different for girls," I say. "Girls who

kiss boys, girls who date them, girls who call them on the phone . . . that's all they do. There are other things I want to do."

"Like go to medical school?" he asks.

I think of my performance in the one-hundred-meter butterfly, of the *caffé* in Italy waiting for me, and of learning how to read *Hamlet* and actually liking it this time.

"That and other things," I say.

I might not ever get a Fulbright and maybe I will hate *Hamlet,* but I like to think about the possibilities. *Privately.*

"You're pretty secretive for a girl," he says.

"What is that, a compliment?"

Francis laughs. "Yes, it is."

"Well, thank you. You're pretty nice for a boy."

"I'm sorry I tried to kiss you," he says.

He's sorry? I don't want him to be sorry. Does that mean he doesn't want to anymore? I suppose it shouldn't matter what he wants, since I'm the clueless idiot who wants her brains more than a boyfriend.

"Friends?" he asks.

"Yes," I say, thinking of Justin and the Wolf Pack and how Henry is the only boy left who I can call my friend. "That would be good."

He holds out his hand and I slip mine into his

for a businesslike shake. He says he'll walk me home across the park and we stop at the Boathouse and spend our remaining four dollars on ice-cream cones. Daddy had his fortieth birthday at the Boathouse. It was a catered sit-down dinner party for sixty people, and there was a string quartet during the cocktails and then a live band for dancing after dinner. I mention this to Francis and he says that sounds like a big fuss for a grown-up's birthday.

When we pass Strawberry Fields, Francis asks what I want to do on Sunday.

"Do we have plans on Sunday?" I ask, realizing that it has been since forever that I have done anything on weekends that wasn't homework- or Daddy-related.

"Of course we do," he says. "How about going to the carousel before it closes for the winter?"

Erhart loved the carousel, I think carefully and deliberately to myself. The wooden painted horses that went round and round never failed to thrill him. I think he would love for me to go with someone who is certainly not my twin, but my friend.

EIGHT

Freddie and I are eating dinner alone at a restaurant on West Fifty-third Street just off Sixth Avenue. Although we have never been to Pronto before, it is not the first time we have eaten three courses (salad, pasta, and dessert) in a strange place while waiting for Daddy. Freddie only eats salad with the dressing served on the side in a small ceramic bowl. She orders dinner and dessert, though, and moves the food around on her plate. It's not a charming sight, and so I stare at the people sitting by the bar while trying to hear what the woman at the next table is saying. It's impossible to tell if the man she is with is her husband or her father.

I wonder if people look at Daddy and Freddie when they are out alone together and wonder that. My sister looks almost exactly like Mother: tall, thin, narrow shoulders, blonde, and blue-eyed. She also looks older than seventeen. Daddy is handsome. There's no way around that. It's easy to see why women *throw themselves* at him. If you didn't know better you might think that Freddie was a young woman out on a date with an older, handsome man.

Since she leaves it cut up into bits on her plate, I eat all of Freddie's lemon tart. My tiramisu tasted like vanilla pudding with something sour mixed in it.

"Maybe we got the night wrong," Freddie says.

My sister's unfailing ability to put a positive light on any and all of Daddy's behavior never fails to amaze me.

"Not likely," I say. "There was a reservation in his name, remember?"

"It's just that he would call if he got caught in a meeting or something."

I am about to ask her when Daddy has ever called to excuse his lateness or even his complete absence, but at that moment I see him being led to the table by a waiter.

"Here you are," he says, as if we had mistakenly gotten separated from him instead of waiting for almost two hours.

The waiter hands Daddy the menu, but he shakes his head, saying that he phoned ahead and the kitchen should have his sautéed baby lamb chops ready by now. I'm glad he called somebody, but wish it had been us. Freddie asks to have a decaf espresso, which I happen to know she hates, but she thinks ordering it makes her grown up. Daddy asks for a glass of Merlot and turns to me.

"How about you, Sophia? Won't you join me by having a little something?"

"We've eaten," I tell him.

"She'd like a Shirley Temple," Freddie says to Daddy, and I wonder if I am going to have to excuse myself to go throw up in the ladies' room.

Shirley Temples are ginger ale mixed with cherry syrup. Freddie knows Erhart and I loved them. We loved the sickly-sweet taste and we loved the color, which was neither gold nor red, but a sort of burnt orange. I've not had a Shirley Temple since Erhart and if I ever do have one again, it won't be in this company.

"So how are my children?" Daddy asks, unfolding his napkin with a great flourish.

It takes all the energy I have not to blurt out *Well, one of them's dead,* so I can't think of an answer.

"Ian got a subscription to the speaker series at the Ninety-second Street Y," Freddie says.

Ian is Freddie's graduate student. The speaker series at the Y is really just a bunch of writers reading from their work and taking questions from the audience. I don't know that she's ever read a book that wasn't assigned for school. If Ian thought about Freddie even a third as much as she thinks about him, he would not be dragging her to the Y.

"He asked how *you* were," I say. "Not what Ian's done."

"I know what he asked," Freddie says.

"And how are you, Sophia?" Daddy asks, nodding his thanks to the waiter who brings the Merlot.

"She's fine," Freddie says. "Straight A's in school. Swim team star. You know the drill."

One of the main reasons I try and avoid these little outings with Daddy is that they don't bring out the best in my sister.

"Actually, I suck at the butterfly and I've missed two deadlines on my English essay."

"Don't say *suck,* Sophia. It sounds so ugly on a woman."

"My performance in the one-hundred-meter butterfly is substandard," I say. "It's not up to snuff. It's weak. Wretched. Horrible. Slow."

"And yet you're having trouble in English," Daddy says as the waiter puts his plate down. "What's this essay on?"

There is a special serrated knife on the plate so that he can more easily cut through the baby lamb chops.

"Time," I say.

"The great cliché," Daddy says, red juice scampering around his plate as one of the chops gives way. "'Time is money.' 'Father Time.' 'Time heals all wounds.' Lord, no wonder you're having trouble. What kind of a jackass assigned such a topic?"

"We picked our own topics," I say.

"So you've made your own bed," Daddy says.

"I suppose," I say, deciding to ignore that he's called me a jackass.

"And how about you, Frederica?" Daddy asks. "What are you reading?"

Probably Cliff Notes, I think, but Freddie sips neatly at her small cup of black sludge before saying, "Ibsen."

Daddy asks what play and then launches into a monologue on the history of theater in Scandinavia. I stop listening at some point, because I am organizing what I know about time as the Great Cliché. Daddy said time is money. What else have people used as a metaphor for time? I'll bet there are a slew of books and poems and even plays about the different theories people have had about time. That could be two whole sections of the essay right there: cliché and metaphor.

How about the way we measure time? In geometry, the shortest distance between two points is a straight line. If I decide that Erhart's dying is one point and my turning twenty-one is another point, then what is the shortest distance between them? In other words, is nine years a line? If so, how do we account for the fact that we have repetitive ways of measuring time, like the months in a year, days in a week, et cetera? Excellent. Section three: Is time a line or a circle?

I am so excited at having enough information to at least pad out an outline that I have lost all track of the conversation and have no idea how Daddy and Freddie arrived at the topic of Nick and Francis. Daddy is asking why they were at the house for dinner.

"I guess Mother wanted us to meet him," Freddie says, shrugging.

"But you said you *had* met him. He had picked Katya up for a date and you had met him then."

Mother's name is Katherine, but Daddy always called her Katya. I used to think it was nice. Now for some reason it bothers me to hear him use that private name for her, as if they still belonged to each other.

"I think Nick wanted to make sure his son approved of us before he and Mother got too serious," I say.

I don't think that this is what happened at

all, though Francis did tell me that when Nick first started dating, he would find out how a woman felt about children ("boys in particular," Francis said) before asking her out.

"That's so not the case," Freddie says.

"Are they serious?" Daddy asks.

"I don't know," I say. "Probably depends on if Francis liked us."

"I hope he didn't," Freddie says. "He was a little crazy."

"This man's son is retarded?"

"His name is Nick," I say.

"No," Freddie says. "Not retarded. Strange. He has a tattoo. On his face."

"Is he in a gang?" Daddy asks.

My father has this way of asking questions that he must already know the answer to, but asks them in order to imagine the worst possible scenario.

"No," I say. "His mother died."

"How is that strange?" Daddy asks me.

As if I were the one who said Francis was strange. I decide to stop answering these questions and try to get him back on Scandinavian theater. Only I don't get a chance because Daddy keeps talking.

"You think death only happened to us? That's not like you, Sophia. I rely on you to use your head a little. Your mind."

Daddy likes to say that I am the child of his mind and Freddie is the child of his heart. I think this is a fancy way of calling Freddie stupid and saying he doesn't love me as much as he loves her. I've often wondered how Freddie feels about being the child of his heart, but I've never had the nerve to ask her. Erhart was his son and as such didn't need a special title.

"I don't think death only happened to us," I say. "I think it's safer to say you forgot it was happening to us *before* it happened."

This is why Daddy moved out: he was having an affair. Mother said that under normal circumstances it would be one thing, but with Erhart dying, Daddy should just pack up and go. Freddie says Mother picked a bad time to overreact. I personally think that bad timing was having an affair while Erhart was in the hospital, but what do I know? I've never kissed anyone, let alone had an affair.

"Oh, God," Freddie says. "Please. Let's not go over that again."

"You're very hard, Sophia," Daddy says, signaling for the check. "Time will be the judge of all our actions. In the end, it will not be up to you who goes to heaven or hell."

When he still lived with us, Daddy had a framed print of a painting by Hieronymus Bosch hanging in his study. It was horrible to look at, with knives going through ears and bloated rodents marching around a skeleton. Daddy said it was a sixteenth-century attempt to depict hell. Hell was much worse than the painting, he told me. Hell was an eternity in the absence of love. *An eternity in the absence of love* was always too vague to think about, but now it's perfect for my essay.

Isn't eternity the whole point of religion? Of heaven and hell? That in due course, in good time, we will all be rewarded? Part four: God and time. The End. When it's my turn to hug Daddy goodbye before getting into the taxi home, I give him a squeeze.

"Thank you," I say. "It was so helpful."

"It's only dinner," he says, handing Freddie a twenty to cover the cab fare.

He'll never understand that it's not the food, but how he makes me think. That he may not love me as much as he does Freddie or the way he loved his son, but I am so very much the child of his mind.

NINE

I am in my room doing homework. More specifically, doing homework in every subject except English. What seemed so clear in the restaurant the other night is now a jumbled mess in my head. Time keeps going on without my producing an essay outline about it.

There's a sharp knock on the door and Freddie sticks her head in.

"Phone for you," she says.

Since last year, the phone has never been for me. Henry is too busy with chess and karate to talk on the phone, and Daddy knows to talk to Freddie instead of me whenever possible.

"Who is it?" I ask.

"Some boy," Freddie says. "Don't talk forever. I'm expecting a call from Ian."

I walk into the living room and remember how every time it was a boy last year, I felt guilty and angry at the same time. It's not a boy, exactly. Or rather, the boy on the phone is Francis.

"Hey, there," he says. "How's it going?"

"Fine," I say, but it comes out sounding more like a question.

It takes me a while to figure out that he hasn't called for any particular reason. We already have plans for Saturday — we're finally going to the Frick. He tells me about his day and how boring his tutor is and about a shop he saw which only sells violins and music scores.

"It was the coolest place," he says. "I couldn't believe such a great store could exist on the Upper East Side."

I refrain from saying I told you so, because I'm glad at how happy he sounds and maybe one day he'll like the neighborhood as much as I do. He asks how my day was and I tell him, leaving out the parts that belong to me. Like how Justin Hawker and I collided outside of the pool locker rooms and neither of us were willing to say sorry. Just picked up our things and stalked away from each other. Or how in Italian class I was so busy thinking about my Fulbright that I didn't hear Mrs. Caccini calling on me.

It doesn't leave much to say, so I wind up telling Francis that *Hamlet* is much easier to understand if I read it aloud than if I read it to myself. It means I can't read it in study hall, but I am liking it better this way.

"Plays are like that," he says. "They were written to be read aloud, so reading them any other way is kind of useless."

He starts to tell me about what a disaster the dinner he made tonight was and then he says, "I should let you go. I know you like to get your homework done."

"It'll get done," I say. "It always does."

"So it's okay to call?"

"Yes," I say. "It's nice to talk to you."

And when we hang up, I realize I was telling the truth. It is always nice to talk to him.

Francis doesn't like the Frick. He says it's too much of a rich person's house. That there's no excuse for anyone to have lived in a home big enough for a front hall with a marble fountain in it.

"Fountains belong outside," he says. "In parks and town squares."

That's totally ridiculous, as I point out to him. "With that kind of reasoning no one should have flowers inside either. And there have been studies done which prove that having something lovely around — like a vase of flowers — improves one's mood."

I read this in an article for a term paper Freddie had to write last year for her biology class. I did all the research for her.

"But anyone can have flowers around," Francis says. "It costs five or six dollars to buy flowers. It costs millions to put a fountain in your front hall."

"There are lots of places where five or six dollars is all anybody earns in a month," I say.

I know this from history class. Totalitarian systems more often than not fail to provide fair economic climates.

"Basically we're arguing about the degree to which people should be allowed to go to make themselves happy," Francis says.

"You're arguing about it," I say. "I'm glad Henry Clay Frick spent millions building himself a fountain. I get to enjoy it for eight dollars."

"That's more than you'd have to spend for flowers," he says.

When my father breaks up with a woman, he sends her three dozen red roses and a card. Talk about a cliché. Those flowers — the breakup ones — cost around two hundred dollars.

I know, because Daddy once told us that leaving women was becoming more expensive than staying with them. When I tell Francis this, I like how he doesn't call my father a jerk, which Henry did. Instead, Francis tucks his hands under his arms before shoving them into his pockets.

"That's an awful thing for you to know," he says. "I'm so sorry."

I shrug like it's no big deal. But what he said follows me all through the museum, and in the picture gallery I point out my favorite picture. Turns out that it's his too.

I get another extension from Mr. Gallagher for my outline. Almost everyone in the class is having to redo theirs, so I guess he feels that he can wait a little longer for a first draft of mine. Henry's outline was returned to him with the comment *Badly researched.*

"How am I supposed to research music?" Henry asks. "The whole point of my essay is that I dislike music because I don't know anything about it."

I tell him about the store on East Eighty-first Street which only sells violins and music scores.

"Maybe someone there could help you," I say. "Francis says the staff are all retired teachers from Juilliard."

"Who is Francis?" Henry asks.

"A friend of mine," I say. "His father is dating my mother."

"Your mother is dating somebody?"

"Yeah," I say.

"Do you like him?" Henry asks.

"I do. Mother really likes him. It's good."

"No," Henry says, in the weary, patient tone he uses on our teachers and classmates. "Francis. Do you like Francis?"

"I told you," I say. "He's a friend of mine."

Finally, in a fit of desperation, I tell Francis about my nonexistent essay outline. How there's this gap between the thoughts in my head and the paper due on Mr. Gallagher's desk next week. He asks if he can hear the thoughts in my head, and I recite the sections I came up with while having dinner with Daddy and Freddie.

"So you have cliché, metaphor, measurement, and God all in one essay about time," Francis says. "That's a lot of stuff to be carrying around in your head."

"Well, I don't know a lot about any of those things," I say.

"Let me ask you something, just so that I'm clear, okay?"

"Sure," I say.

"Don't get mad," he says.

"I won't," I say. "Ask anything you want."

"Why aren't you even mentioning your brother? Time and death are two things you know a lot about."

"They aren't things I want to write about," I say. "Let alone turn in for a grade."

"What if you wrote out the four sections you've thought of and included stuff about Erhart in each section?"

I notice how it doesn't sound shocking to hear Francis say my brother's name. And that what he is saying makes a lot of sense. After all, the time between Erhart's dying and now is the only time I'm interested in measuring, no matter if it's a line or a circle.

"Mr. Gallagher is not someone I want reading private stuff," I say.

"You write the private stuff to help you get your thoughts out of your head and into an outline," Francis says. "You can take it out before you hand it in."

"That's a really good idea," I say. "Thanks."

"You're welcome," he says.

We are sitting on the front steps of the Metropolitan Museum, which is where we usually meet. There's a pale ray of sunshine stretching toward us. I know that in a minute we will get up and walk to a coffee shop a few blocks away. Or we might go downtown to look around in another neighborhood. It will be a good afternoon. One of many. I catch my breath in wonder at the thought.

TEN

Francis really likes the outline I finally do, as does Mr. Gallagher, who returns it with a note saying, "Well worth the wait, Sophie. I knew you had it in you. Keep it up." Francis consults with Nick and draws up a five-page reading list of books which discuss the nature of time. The list is organized into sections: literature, philosophy, science, and religion. In history one morning, instead of giving my notes to Henry, I accidentally pass him my outline and the reading list.

During the break, Henry asks if I've lost my mind.

"Not that I'm aware of," I say. "Why?"

"This is the best example I've ever seen of sloppy thinking," Henry says, holding up my outline as if it were an article of really dirty laundry.

"How do you figure?" I ask.

"First of all, you've missed completely that

religion and time are connected by how religion measures time."

"That's in part four."

"Eternity is in part four, not religion," Henry says. "It's only Christianity that thinks time is eternal. A straight line. Eastern religions think of time as a circle."

"Well, I have a section on how we measure time," I say.

I can't believe Henry is this angry about my homework.

"No, you have some muddled thinking on how we measure time," he says. "Our time measurements, which are circular, come from certain scientific laws. The earth revolves around the sun, thus the seasons."

"I am aware that the earth revolves around the sun, Henry" I say. "But it doesn't explain everything about how we measure time."

"Your outline has also neglected the psychology of time, which I can explain," he says.

The bell rings, but neither of us moves.

"By all means," I say. "Please do."

"Linear time comes from man's need to shape random events into order. People can't accept that bad things happen, so they resort to cause-and-effect theories, which leads to linear time."

Henry looks and sounds both smug and

angry. I have never seen him this bent out of shape.

"What makes you the first and last authority on time?" I ask.

"I know more than your boyfriend who drew up this totally incoherent reading list," Henry says.

Boyfriend?

"What are you talking about? I don't have a boyfriend."

"I don't care what you call that guy," Henry says. "The wack with the tear."

Francis. This is about Francis. How could Henry possibly think Francis is my boyfriend? I snatch the reading list out of Henry's hands.

"It's a tattoo of a tear," I say. "I only told you about it because of the guys in your karate class."

"I'm sorry," Henry says. "The wack with the tattoo who does your homework."

"Francis didn't help me with this. His father did. His award-winning professor of history father," I say. "I very much doubt it's incoherent."

"Well, I very much doubt that you'll be able to write a decent essay now that you're an A-girl," Henry says. "Before the tattoo, you would never have let somebody else do your homework for you. Never."

He drops my outline on the ground and walks back into the classroom. I sit down on the bottom step of the stairwell. It's hard to catch my breath and harder to see without everything blurring. At first I think I'm going to throw up, and then I realize I'm crying. How dare he? How dare he?

Henry has a chess tutor. They meet every night and play for two hours. It's to ensure that Henry never gets stale or content or bored, the way he might if he were studying on his own. In addition to his regular karate classes, he has a private session on Saturday mornings. Every day I give him a chance to copy my notes.

I have never thought less of Henry because of the help he gets. Have never once thought that he was as low as a Wolf Pack member. Justin Hawker and his new friends can't do anything on their own. They seem to need each other's help for everything. I'm always surprised that Justin can come to swim practice without his pals following him into the pool.

How dare Henry yell at me for getting help in a class he knows I'm not doing well in? I am not an A-girl. Or am I? I take a deep breath, pick up the papers Henry has thrown at me, and stand up. Of course I don't have a boyfriend — don't even want one — but I do think about Francis a lot. We talk on the phone almost every night and I skip afternoon practice twice a week so he and I can hang out.

I've thought a lot about that afternoon when I didn't let Francis kiss me. Often, I've wished that I had. There's something about being with Francis that makes my skin itch to touch him. Maybe the wanting is as bad for me as the doing. If Henry can think I've turned into an A-girl because I might have a crush on a boy, imagine what he would think of me if I definitely liked Francis that way all the time. Instead of just sometimes and in secret.

I decide not to use Nick's reading list. I'll go to the library on my own. Ask Mr. Gallagher. Or Mother. Or, God help me, Daddy.

During English, Henry and I sit far apart, and when class is over I ask Mr. Gallagher about revising my reading list. He says the one I've already shown him looks fine. He wouldn't have anything to add to it. Or subtract, for that matter.

"Well, what if I don't want to use that list?"

"Sophie, it's a free-form essay. Not a research paper. You don't have to do any reading."

So not helpful. As if I have, stored in my brain, an encyclopedia on religion. Not to mention metaphor, cliché, and not only how but why we measure time the way we do.

"Have you considered exploring your own thoughts on time?" Mr. Gallagher asks me. "How you feel about time. Personally."

This is Mr. Gallagher's first year at Tyler Prep. There are a lot of things he doesn't know about me. Breaking in a new teacher is imperative, but not always pleasant.

"I'm going to medical school," I tell him. "I'm more concerned with how things work than in how things feel."

"I see," says Mr. Gallagher.

"So I'll need some reading suggestions," I say. "Because my essay will be on how time works. Not on how I feel about it."

"How things feel is connected to how things work," he says. "You know that, don't you?"

I nod, but I'm only humoring him. Breaking in a teacher takes a fair amount of agreeing with inaccuracies. How things feel has little to no impact on how things work. For example, every illness known to man has its own system. Leukemia has its own internal logic that maps out a plan of attack.

My feelings about the illness don't change how it works. Maybe no one Mr. Gallagher loves has ever died. I am only fifteen years old. Who am I to explain to him just how leukemia worked on Erhart and how I felt about it. Feel about it, I correct myself. And yet, I know that I think differently about Erhart's illness now than I did when I was twelve.

"Yes," I say, standing up. "Of course. Yes. Thank you."

I don't know if I agree or disagree with him, but there is an essay I can write without research. A personal essay about the gap between felt and feel when it comes to leukemia.

ELEVEN

After school, I meet Francis at the coffee shop we go to when it's raining or too cold to walk around outside. When it's nice out, we meet in front of the Metropolitan Museum, which we still haven't gone into, and walk downtown to Gramercy Park. If I feel like it, we head west to Sixth Avenue and down a bit to Eighteenth Street, where there are three used bookstores Francis loves.

Some days, we head back east and go even further downtown until we get to Tompkins Square Park. Francis says that the city once tried to set the park on fire as a way of forcing the homeless to leave the area. I'm pretty sure that it didn't happen that way, but it's always interesting to hear what Francis has to say about the city as we walk through it. Today it is drizzling and even though Francis prefers to *do things,* I just want to sit and stare out the window.

"You know, I think your mom is going to come with us at Christmas," Francis says, pouring about a mile of sugar into his tea.

He and Nick are going to Meadowbrooke for a visit. Mother told me that Nick thinks Francis is homesick. And lonely.

"I know," I say.

This year, Freddie and I are supposed to spend Christmas with Daddy. That's assuming, of course, that he can work us into his schedule. Joy, joy, joy.

"Hey, you in there," Francis says, waving a napkin in front of me. "What's going on?"

"I had a bad day," I say.

"Homework or friends?"

"Both," I say, smiling at the waitress who puts a plate of pancakes in front of Francis and a blueberry muffin in front of me.

As far as I can tell, Francis and his tutor never eat lunch. I have never seen anybody eat as much in one afternoon as Francis does. He is always starving.

"So what happened?" he asks, pouring syrup all over his plate.

Because I am now in the habit of telling Francis the truth, I have already prepared a heavily edited version of what Henry said. I give the basic facts, but leave out the part about

Henry calling Francis my boyfriend. Francis listens intently while eating bite after bite of pancakes.

"He called you an A-girl because Nick and I drew up that list?"

"Yes."

"I thought A-girls were girls with boyfriends," Francis says.

"Or girls who want boyfriends," I say. "They're also girls who are dumb. Girls who aren't interested in . . . themselves."

"I know," Francis says. "They have no focus."

"That's the Wolf Pack," I say. "A-girls have some focus."

"But it's on boys," Francis says. "And Henry called you an A-girl because he thinks you're spending too much time with me. He thinks that if you had done your own reading list, you would be less focused on me."

"It doesn't have anything to do with you," I say. "It has to do with what Henry said. I know it's stupid, but it was insulting."

"How do you think real A-girls feel?"

I break off an edge of muffin. I can see where Francis is going here, but there's no way to block it. Best not to answer and get this over with as quickly as possible. I know Francis doesn't approve of Henry. Says he sounds arrogant. Even for a genius.

"You two have the school all neatly divided up into A-girls and Wolf Packs," Francis says. "Has it occurred to you that there are real people under those labels? And that you make them feel stupid?"

"They are stupid," I say. "I don't make them that way."

"What makes them stupid?" Francis asks me, folding his hands under his arms. "What is it, exactly, that you and Henry have against people who go on dates?"

"Never mind," I say. "It's not that simple. And I really don't need another lecture right now."

"Justin Hawker is stupid?"

"How do you know who Justin Hawker is?" I ask him, really freaked out to hear Francis talking about Justin, who is not, in any way, stupid.

"You'll be mad," Francis says.

"No, I'll be interested. How do you know Justin?"

"I asked Nick to ask your mother if you had ever had a boyfriend," he says, taking the bottom half of my muffin. "She told him that you used to be best friends with one Justin Hawker, but that you blew him off last year."

"That's only partly accurate," I say.

I am too afraid to ask him why he asked Nick to ask about my ever having had a boyfriend. I am afraid because I know the answer has to do with whether or not Francis likes me. And whether or not I like him. As more than friends.

"Is he stupid?" Francis asks. "Did you blow him off because he was stupid?"

"He blew me off," I say. "He was my best friend."

As I say this, I remember that Justin Hawker was the only person from school whom I asked to Erhart's funeral. He brought me yellow tulips. I kept them in my room for almost two months.

"Henry's smart," Francis says.

"He's a genius," I say, wondering if I do like Francis or if I just miss Justin. Miss how easy everything used to be.

"He's never tried to kiss you, has he?"

"Henry?" I ask, grossed out beyond belief. "Of course not."

"I'd like to meet him," Francis says.

"He thinks I'm an A-girl because of you. I don't think I need the two of you meeting."

Henry thinks I'm a moron because of Francis and Francis thinks I'm judgmental because of

Henry. What is it about friends that gives them the right to have so many opinions?

"You know, I had a girlfriend at Meadowbrooke," Francis says. "You would have thought she was an A-girl."

He had a girlfriend? Or he has one still, but she's far away? Do I care? No, I guess not. Justin dates one of the A-girls at school, and if Henry went on a date I don't think I would care as long as he still sat with me at lunch.

"We broke up," Francis says.

"Well, you were moving," I say.

Daddy had a girlfriend in California once. And one in Chicago. He had to get rid of them, he told us. They were geographically undesirable.

"No," Francis says. "We broke up because she was boring."

I try not to smile, but can feel one fighting to break out. I look down at the remains of my muffin.

"I made her feel bad," Francis says. "And she bored me."

"What was her name?" I ask.

"Alicia."

We smile at each other and then he starts to laugh. Really hard in that contagious way that makes you mortified and happy all at the same time.

"My real name is Anna Sophia Maria," I say when we have calmed down.

"I don't know," Francis says. "I don't see how you could possibly turn into an A-girl. Even if you dated me, Henry, and Justin."

"Justin doesn't talk to me anymore," I say.

"Neither does Henry now," Francis points out.

"Maybe you should meet him," I say. "Henry might like you better if he knew you."

"Maybe Justin would talk to you if you talked to him," Francis says.

"I very much doubt it," I say.

"Justin's not a criminal, you know. He just wanted to go on a date."

There's something about the tone of Francis's voice, about the way his very green eyes are fixed on me, that makes me nervous. No matter what Henry thinks, I'm not stupid. I know Francis is talking about something other than Justin and Henry. Other than Alicia. We've been having a conversation about dating. Only, I have no idea how I fit into Francis's ideas about dating. And worse, I have no idea how he fits into mine.

TWELVE

At practice the next afternoon, Justin and I wind up in the same lane. Coach Alden has decided that we all need to work on our weakest event. Justin and I both suck at the backstroke. I suppose that in deference to Daddy I should say that we are substandard, not up to snuff, weak, wretched, horrible, and very slow.

Justin and I are the only ones on the team whose weakest link is the backstroke. The butterfly lane is the most crowded. Then the breaststroke. In the backstroke, a good back flip at the turn, which neither of us can do, really helps. There's a flag hanging from the ceiling about fifteen yards in from either end of the pool, and you're supposed to count from the flag to the wall so that you don't crack your head. I'm exactly three and a half strokes between the flag and the wall, but Justin can't figure out where he is in relation to the wall. His whole workout is like bang, turn, swim, bang, and turn again.

We're both so slow that we finish up a set just as the next set is starting. Coach Alden tells us to wait until the rest of the team is done. So we stand in the shallow end. I can't speak for Justin, but I'm freezing, tired, and sluggish. He takes his goggles off and presses the back of his head with the palms of his hands.

"I guess we should have done our essays on the backstroke," I say.

"How do you know I didn't?" he asks.

"I don't," I say and then, after a pause, "Did you?"

"No," Justin says. "If I'd known we were going to have to write an entire essay on what we dislike, I would have picked something different though."

"What did you pick?" I ask.

"What did you pick, Sophie?" he asks, his voice hostile and defensive as if I've asked him something really personal.

"Time," I says.

"Time," he says, with a laugh that sounds like a barking seal. "Time. Man, that's worse than mine. What do you dislike about time?"

"It passes," I say. "Things change. They're not always good changes. I don't know."

"That's good," Justin says. "You can get a decent essay out of that. I picked money."

"My father says time is money," I say, remembering how Daddy unwittingly called me a jackass.

"Mine says money is the only thing that matters," Justin says.

And then I think about what happened to Justin about a year after Erhart died. The year before Justin joined the Wolf Pack. His parents got divorced and because Justin's father makes so much money, there was a big fight in court over who lived with whom and how much money would go where. It was in the newspaper. Mrs. Hawker had a really famous lawyer. The court ordered Mr. Hawker to build a small house behind his huge one in Forest Hills, which is a neighborhood in Queens for rich people. Justin's parents take turns living in the smaller house so that the kids can stay put. I can see how money would have made that divorce easy for Justin and yet awful at the same time.

"I'm sorry," I say.

Justin spits into his goggles before submerging them in the water.

"What the hell are you sorry for?" he asks.

What am I sorry for? That I never wanted to go on a date? That I made him feel bad? That he dates an A-girl now? No, that's not it. I'm sorry his father thinks money is the only thing that matters. I'm sorry I don't know how to tell Justin exactly how much I know about fathers and what matters to them. I'm sorry we got older without staying friends. Sorry we are now so bad at talking to each other that even time between sets is strained. The rest of the team is finishing up the set we have been sitting out.

"I don't know," I say. "Nothing, I guess."

"That figures," Justin says, snapping his goggles into place.

The whistle blows and we take off, doing the other thing we're both bad at.

I have dinner alone because Mother has gone out with Nick, and Freddie is at the 92nd Street Y with Ian. Before Mother met Nick, the only nights I would have the apartment to myself were when Mother was out of town for work and Daddy was supposed to have us over but would forget or cancel. Freddie always took advantage of those nights by staying out late with her friends. I would spend the entire evening terrified that Mother would call and find out that not only had Daddy screwed up again, but that Freddie was breaking her curfew.

Tonight I take a bag of marshmallows and a

jar of peanut butter into the dining room. There's no chocolate or even graham crackers in the house so I have to settle for Saltines. I light the candles and pretend that I am eating s'mores. Erhart loved them. He and I used to powder our faces with marshmallows. Neither of us were particularly interested in makeup, but we liked the idea of eating something that looked like it could be used for something so removed from food.

In the hospital, he once had hot chocolate with mini-marshmallows in it. He said only a hospital would take a perfect food and shrink it. He didn't believe Mother when she said that you could get them that way out of the hospital too. The next day, we brought a bag of mini-marshmallows over. Erhart was so excited to see that they were real and not some evil hospital invention. When I think about all the things he never did learn, it makes me feel as if I could cry for nine months and not ever be finished.

At first, I tried to keep a list of all the new things I learned so that I could figure out just how much Erhart missed by dying. It quickly got too long and too confusing. I don't like to eat cow glands, which I found out the hard way by ordering sweetbreads at a restaurant once. Was discovering that sweetbreads were nasty-tasting cow glands a new thing or an old thing which I hadn't known about before he died? I couldn't decide. And anyway, it wasn't going to make my brother any less dead if I kept a list of everything his dying kept him from discovering.

I blow the candles out. Eating in the dining room isn't necessarily the best place for me. I pop one last cracker in my mouth and gather up the junk I've covered the table with. When the phone rings, I assume it's Francis, who will be annoyed when he discovers that I've not spoken to Henry about the three of us getting together. Henry and I avoided each other like the plague all day long.

It's not Francis, but Daddy on the phone, and he is not that concerned with how my day was. In fact, he thinks I'm Freddie. Once we get that straightened out, he asks to speak to Mother.

"She's out with Nick," I say.

"Still?"

"Again," I say. "She comes home between dates."

"This has been going on a long time, no?"

"Two or three months," I say. "Maybe a little more. They're spending Christmas together."

"Look, Sophia, that's why I'm calling. I'm going to be in Italy on Christmas. You girls will have to stay with Katya."

"She'll be with Nick," I say. "And we already have plans with them for Thanksgiving so if you cancel Christmas, we don't have a holiday with you this year."

We don't actually have plans for Thanksgiving, but there is no way I'm going to let him screw up Mother's Christmas.

"There's always New Year's," Daddy says.

Like he's going to give up New Year's Eve for us. He totally means New Year's Day, when all his friends are hung over.

"That counts as next year," I say. "You'd better skip Italy."

"Sophia, I have very little control over my schedule," Daddy says, sounding as defensive and hostile as Justin did at practice. "Guido has a concert in Florence on Christmas day."

Daddy has two jobs. One for money and one for love. The one for money is writing music for commercials. The one for love is as an accompanist for Guido Lappani, who is a really famous tenor even though he isn't one of the Three Tenors. If you know a lot about tenors, which most people don't, Guido is famous. And he and Daddy travel everywhere that people want to hear Guido sing.

I'd be way more impressed with Daddy having two jobs if he hadn't taken the one for love the minute Erhart got sick. I was only ten, but I could use a dictionary. I figured out pretty fast that *acute leukemia* meant my brother was dying, even though I wasn't sure what dying meant. Except that it was bad. It was bad enough for Mother to stop working and for Daddy to start a job for love, which required even more travel than the job for money did.

"It sounds like you'll be skipping us," I say. "A-plus in the Daddy department."

"This is ridiculous," Daddy says. "Good parenting doesn't only involve holidays."

Good parenting? What did he do? Read a how-to book?

"What *does* good parenting involve?" I ask.

"Being involved," he says. "Interested in who you are and what you do."

I decide to test this theory of his on him.

"I have a big swim meet right before Thanksgiving," I say. "You want to come?"

It will either be work or a girl, I think, but my father does the unexpected. The undesired, if truth be told.

"Yes," he says. "I would love that. You swim the one-hundred-meter backstroke, right?

"Butterfly," I say. "It's not that big a deal. You really shouldn't feel obliged to come."

"I don't feel at all obliged," Daddy says. "I'm thrilled to be invited. Do you realize how long it's been since you've asked me to do anything? Anything at all?"

Let's see now, do I know how long? Two years, five months, and seventeen days.

"Not exactly," I say. "I'll have Mother call you about Christmas and stuff."

"Maybe she could change her Thanksgiving plans," Daddy says. "I'd hate to not be there for you two holidays in a row."

"Don't worry," I say. "It's only Freddie who's going to be bummed if we don't see you for any of the holidays."

"And me," Daddy says. "I'll be quite distraught if I can't see you girls."

Oh, sure. Quite. I give him the swim meet information and bring our chat to a speedy conclusion. I go back to the dining room and relight the candles. Watching the blue part of the flame dance around, I wonder about those two years, five months, and seventeen days. How is it that during that particular passage of time, be it linear or circular, I have neglected to ask my father to do anything? Anything at all?

What is it about the way I am getting older that has caused me to lose my best friend to the Wolf Pack and my father to his own separate life? I sit in the dining room for a really long time. I am still sitting there when Mother comes back from her date. I wave to her through the dining room's glass doors so she won't think there's anything wrong.

"Hello, there," she says, sitting down at the table. "Isn't this romantic."

I look around the room. With the large empty chairs casting flickering shadows, it is romantic. Especially with Mother's face all glowing. Even in the dark, you can tell how happy she is because of Nick.

I give her Daddy's message.

"Well, we'll work something out," she says. "Maybe Nick and I can go to Meadowbrooke at Thanksgiving, instead of Christmas."

"Won't he mind?" I ask.

"Who?"

"Nick. Won't he mind having to change all his plans around because of Daddy?"

"I don't think so," Mother says. "He knows that you and Freddie are important to me and that Fredrich is important to the two of you. Nick's a little more flexible than you are."

This is Mother's big complaint about me: I'm not flexible enough. The focus which Henry admires so much, Mother finds rigid. She thinks it's terrific that I do so well in school, but she thinks too much of anything — even discipline — can be bad.

"Do you think Daddy is a good parent?" I ask.

Mother looks at me. She leans over and

snuffs out the candles with her fingers. Then she gets up and turns on the lights.

"Can you say that again?" she asks me.

"You heard me the first time," I say. "Do you think Daddy is a good parent?"

"I think that what's important here is whether *you* think Daddy is a good parent," she says.

"What if I don't?"

"Then you need to let him know that."

"Okay," I say, standing up.

I give her a kiss good night.

"I'm glad you had a nice time with Nick," I say.

"I am too," she says, and then, "Sophie, he loves you. Try to remember that."

I know she means Daddy and not Nick. But I also know that loving me doesn't mean my father can remember what event I swim or how very different I sound from my sister on the phone.

THIRTEEN

Francis is unimpressed by my inability to arrange a way for him and Henry to meet. Instead of meeting in front of the museum, he says that he will pick me up outside of school.

"That way it will be natural for us to talk," Francis says. "It'll be like an accidental meeting. He's leaving school and I'm waiting for you."

"There's nothing natural about your coming all the way crosstown," I say. "Henry will know it's a setup."

"It's better than waiting for you to start talking to him again," Francis says.

"Why are you so anxious to meet him?" I ask.

"Why are you so anxious to keep us apart?"

"I'm not anxious to keep you apart," I say. "I'm just not anxious for you to meet. There's a difference."

"Are you embarrassed?"

"About what?" I ask, knowing I am embarrassed about so many things that Francis will have to be more specific.

"Me," he says. "Are you embarrassed that you are friends with me? It wouldn't be the first time. People get totally freaked by the tattoo."

"I love the tattoo," I say. "I am so not embarrassed about you."

"Good," he says. "What time should I meet you?"

"School ends at 3:05," I say.

"I'll be outside," he says.

"Okay," I say.

"Sophie, do you really love the tattoo?"

The tattoo forces everyone to deal with Francis's mother. With the fact that once she was alive and now she's dead. It forces Francis to remember his mother every time he looks in the mirror. And it's a terrific symbol for how crying never really ends even if the tears do.

"Yes," I say. "I do."

"I'm glad," he says.

We say goodbye and when I put the phone down I notice that my hands are shaking. I review what I know about idiomatic expressions in Italian. Last night's physics problems. The use of force in governing systems. My hands calm down. All I said was that I loved the tattoo.

* * *

At lunch, Henry and I have continued to sit together (who else would we sit with?) but we have not talked. At all. Very pleasant. Today, Henry hands me an envelope.

"What's this?"

"An apology," he says. "I wasn't very nice about your friend's outline."

"Reading list," I say. "I did my own outline."

"Either way, I behaved badly and it's been cluttering my mind."

Henry's chess tutor is a big believer in having an uncluttered mind. His name is Christopher Cartwright and his basic rule for chess students is that they have no friends. If Henry goes ahead and breaks that rule, he should at least try and think about his friends (i.e., me) as little as possible. I wonder if Francis's tutor has rules. Wonder why I am surrounded by strange boys with tutors. I look down at the envelope.

"You wrote your apology?"

"It's more precise that way. If you'd prefer one in person, you should let me know."

I open the envelope. The apology is typed: *Dear Sophie, I apologize for making derogatory remarks about your friend's facial marks. What people do to their skin is their own personal business. I'm also sorry for degrading the quality of your schoolwork. It really wasn't my place. Please pardon me. Cordially, Henry.*

"Did you write this or did Christopher?"

Henry is in the middle of breaking his five Oreos in half. He looks at me and then back down at his cookies.

"I told him you would be able to tell," he says.

"An A-girl could tell that you didn't write this," I say. "Why does Christopher even know about Francis's tattoo?"

"I've been playing horribly all week," Henry says. "He has to know what's going on in my life if it affects my chess."

"Fighting with me has been making you play bad chess?"

Henry nods.

"Well, I accept your apology," I say. "Even if it's from Christopher."

"Thank you," Henry says.

"You know how strange you are, right?"

Henry looks across the cafeteria where Justin Hawker and the Wolf Pack are sitting at a table right next to a bunch of A-girls.

"Considering the alternatives," he says, "I don't think I'm so badly off."

Then he tells me that he has to leave school after English for a doctor's appointment and would I please hand in his physics assignment. I put his assignment and his apology in my book bag. I will give the apology to Francis. Once he's read it he will know Henry a lot better than he would by their "accidentally" running into each other.

FOURTEEN

Francis is late. I stand outside the school building, watching people leave in groups. They hang around to say their extended goodbyes before separating to go home. This is a part of school I miss by heading to the pool every day. At three-thirty, Francis has still not shown up and almost everyone has gone. It's just me and Justin's A-girl standing around. Her name's Rebecca Goldman and she's pretty much what you think of when you think of what a girl should look like: clean, properly curved, polished, and carefully dressed.

I hug my old coat around me. I have on a long flowered skirt that used to be Freddie's and a sweater I saved from Mother's giveaway pile. Rebecca has on a short blue-jean skirt, black tights, black loafers, and a black turtleneck. Her coat is camel-haired. None of the buttons are loose. Her hair is straight and it gleams, a kind of blondish brown.

"Hey," she says. "You waiting?"

No, I'm just standing out here on the sidewalk because the view's so great.

"Yes," I say.

"Me too," she says.

I had kind of figured that.

"Who are you waiting for?" she asks.

"A friend of mine," I say.

"Oh," she says.

I look down the street, away from her and her polished gleam.

"I'm waiting for Justin," she says.

I look at my watch: 3:32. Hard to believe only two minutes have gone by since we started talking. Feels like an hour.

"Practice doesn't get out until 4:45," I say. "You've got kind of a long wait."

"He skipped practice," she says. "He had to see Mr. Kelley."

I can believe that. Justin was never very good at math.

"He told me about your essay," she says, pulling a strand of her hair away from her lipsticked mouth. "It sounds really interesting. You'll never believe what I picked to write about."

"Actually, we picked what we disliked most," I say. "At the time, we didn't know we were going to have to write about it."

"Right," Rebecca says. "The paragraph."

"So what do you dislike?" I ask.

"Eggs," she says. "My whole life I've hated to eat eggs and my mother made them for breakfast every day."

"You have to write a five-page essay on eggs?"

"Mr. Gallagher said that it sounded to him that I disliked being forced to eat something more than I disliked the eggs," Rebecca says. "He said I could do an essay on how I dislike authority, but it's the eggs."

"You'd rather write an essay on eggs than on authority?"

"Oh, sure," she says. "But I like your topic better."

"I've always liked eggs," I say.

"Justin says your essay will be way more interesting than mine."

I see Francis heading toward the school in a dead run. I see Justin coming out of the school's front entrance. I ignore both of them and take a good look at the beautiful girl in front of me.

"Justin's a jerk," I say. "I think your essay will be very interesting. Quirky and different."

"Hey," Justin says to me, putting his arm around Rebecca.

Francis has slowed to a very fast walk and he approaches us with a smile that reminds me of Nick.

"There was an accident at Fifth Avenue," he says. "They closed off the park."

"It's okay," I say. "Let's go."

Francis and Justin are staring at each other.

"Hey," Rebecca says to Francis. "Are you Sophie's friend?"

Francis nods.

"She's been waiting for you," Rebecca tells him, in case he didn't know that already.

"I'm Francis Roberts," Francis says, holding his hand out.

Rebecca shakes his hand.

"I love your tattoo," she says. "It's so there."

"I'm Justin Hawker," Justin says.

He and Francis shake hands. We're all having a little party here on the sidewalk. Francis looks at me.

"Are you mad?"

"No, I'm cold," I say.

"We're going to the West Cafe," Rebecca says. "You want to come?"

"Thanks, no," I say.

"Sure," Francis says. "That sounds great."

"We have to go," I say to Rebecca. "But thanks."

"We don't have to go anywhere," Francis says. "Come on, let's get something to eat. I'm starved."

And dead, I think to myself. I'm going to kill him.

"Come on, Sophie," Justin says. "Let's celebrate not being in the pool."

They all turn and start heading down the block. And so I follow. We get a booth at the West Cafe. Justin and Francis both order omelettes. I look at Rebecca and we laugh. When I tell Francis what Rebecca's essay is on, he goes up to the counter and changes his order.

"Nice guy," Rebecca says.

"I like eggs," Justin says.

"You like money too," she says. "You just don't like your father."

I wonder if she's a little smarter than I realize. Francis comes back with a cup of tea, which he puts in front of me.

"Here. Drink up. I know you're freezing."

Justin asks Francis where he goes to school.

"I don't. I get tutored."

"Are you a genius like Henry?" Rebecca asks him, and then, before he can answer, she asks me, "Do you only like geniuses or something?"

"Henry is not a genius," Justin says. "He has like the worst grades."

"No," Francis says. "My father can't afford private school and he doesn't think much of the public school system here."

"Francis and his father just moved here," I say.

"What about your mother?" Rebecca asks. "Where does she live?"

Francis touches the tattoo on his face. I don't think he even realizes that he's doing it.

"She's dead," he says.

"Oh, that's terrible," Rebecca says. "I'm so sorry. How awful. I'm so very sorry. I had no idea."

"It's okay," Francis says. "How would you know if you didn't ask?"

"Is that how you met Sophie?" Justin asks.

"Is what how we met?" Francis asks, still smiling at Rebecca, who looks like she wants to crawl under the table.

"You know, with your mother being dead and her brother and all."

I could just smack him. He barely knew Erhart. How dare he bring him up in conversation? In front of Rebecca, who is new this year and has no idea that I ever had a brother? Or so I think.

"You know," Justin says. "Like in a grief support group?"

Francis laughs.

"My mother died when I was eight," he says. "Little late for me to be in grief support, and Sophie's not into that kind of public discussion."

I look at Justin, who is staring at Francis's tattoo the way I did the night I met him.

"His father is dating my mother," I say. "We did not meet because of Erhart."

"But you weren't totally wrong," Francis says to Justin. "After all, if my mother hadn't died, we probably wouldn't have met."

"So you two aren't dating?" Rebecca says.

"No, they're not," Justin says.

Francis looks from me to Justin and back again to me.

"We're friends," I say to Rebecca.

"So are you dating Henry?" Rebecca asks.

"No," I say. "Henry is my best friend."

I glare at Justin. My best friend who is still speaking to me.

"She's not dating anyone," Francis says. "She doesn't approve of it."

"That's so cool," Rebecca says. "How come?"

"It's sort of private," I say.

Our food arrives. Francis has gotten — surprise — pancakes. Rebecca and I have each ordered a muffin, except that hers is chocolate chip and mine is cranberry.

"What's private about it?" Rebecca asks. "Dating is like so public."

"*Why* she doesn't date," Justin says. "That's what is private." ·

Francis asks Rebecca why she doesn't like eggs, and as Justin eats his omelette, she tells us everything she has learned about the poultry industry and how chickens are mistreated in order to lay the most amount of eggs possible. When we get the check both Francis and Justin make a grab for it, but Rebecca snaps it up between her slender fingers.

"This is on me," she says. "It's not every day I get treated to such stimulating company."

Rebecca puts twenty dollars on the table and excuses herself to go to the ladies' room. Francis offers to take the bill up to the counter.

"She's nice," I say to Justin, and I'm surprised to realize I mean it.

Rebecca Goldman, class A-one A-girl, is nice. Who would have thought?

"She is pretty nice," he says. "It's nice you like her."

We look at each other and manage to smile. The effort is more obvious than the smile.

"That boyfriend of yours does not like me," Justin says.

"He's not my boyfriend," I say.

"It's no difference to me," Justin says. "It's

good to see you. You know, good to talk outside of the pool."

"It is," I say.

Rebecca and Francis are conferring at the counter about the tip. He takes five dollars out of his wallet and gives it to her. Francis is a big-time overtipper.

"He likes you enough," I say to Justin.

"He'd like me more if you would date him," Justin says.

"Really?" I ask.

Can that possibly be true? If Francis likes me and has found a way not to be a jerk about it, can't I find a way to like him without being a bore? Without turning into someone who would *choose* eggs over authority as an essay topic?

"I forgot how stupid you can be for a smart girl," Justin says, standing up and gathering the coats into a pile.

I look up at him, prepared to go to war over the word "stupid," but Justin has a real smile on his face. He looks the way he used to before. Not just before Erhart, but before the divorce and the Wolf Pack and my own stupidity.

"It's hard," I say.

"You make it hard," Justin says. "Give him a break. It's that simple."

I get my bag and coat while Justin says his

goodbyes. He and Rebecca leave together. Francis says he'll walk me home. He says he knows I want to kill him. Says he's sorry, but it was just too good an opportunity to pass up. Says he likes Justin. And Rebecca reminds him of Alicia.

"How?" I ask, feeling cold in a way that no amount of hot tea can cure.

"The way she looks, I guess," he says. "A lot of hair. A lot of chitchat. Eggs, God. What was she thinking?"

A lot of hair. My hair is dark like Daddy's, but with Mother's out-of-control curls. Erhart and I both always wore our hair really short because it snarls so easily. Because of swimming and having no patience for blow-dryers, mine's still really short. There's nothing wrong with the way I look, but only girls like Freddie (tall, blonde, cheekbones, and blue eyes) can afford to pay as little attention as I do to the way they look. I would look a lot better if I spent as much time as Rebecca does on her clothes, her make-up, and her hair.

"So you have, like, a type?" I ask, super casual. "You know, a type of girl?"

"We've established that," he says. "Didn't I say Alicia was an A-girl?"

And didn't he say that I could never, ever turn into an A-girl? Maybe Justin's right and I do make it hard. But maybe it's just hard. Hard to know what to do about a boy you'd like to kiss and hit at the same time.

FIFTEEN

Nick has no problem with going to Meadowbrooke at Thanksgiving instead of at Christmas. The problem is Freddie. Ian has invited her to a house party in upstate New York that weekend. She says she could cheerfully kill Daddy.

"There's no way I would have let you go away for the weekend with Ian," Mother says.

"Why not?"

"Ian's twenty-five years old, Freddie. You are not eighteen yet. End of conversation."

"That's not the point," Freddie says. "The point is, I made plans around what I thought Daddy's plans were."

"This is an issue you need to take up with your father," Mother says.

"No, this has to do with you. If you put your foot down, he wouldn't be able to do this."

"What in your life has ever happened to

make you think I have that kind of influence over your father?"

Freddie is silent. What indeed? His affairs? His complete and utter lack of consideration for any of us?

"There's no reason to get so upset over this," Mother says. "Either way, you aren't going away with Ian and you'll still see your father for one of the holidays."

"I just want to be a priority," Freddie says.

"You are a priority," Mother says. "You girls are my life."

"Not for you," Freddie says. "For him."

"Freddie," I say, truly shocked and horrified that she would say such a thing.

Mother looks like my sister has just smacked her across the face.

"That's not what I mean," Freddie says. "I know I'm a priority for you. Daddy's going to one of Sophie's swim meets. Every time Sophie skips out on dinner with him, he spends the entire night talking about her."

"He does?" I say. "You never told me that."

"Freddie, your father is completely secure that you love him. He's less certain about your sister."

"He is?" I say. "Daddy knows I love him."

Doesn't he? I try to recall the last time I

might have told him so. The last time we had a conversation that didn't involve a lot of effort to stay pleasant. I can't. Talking to my father has become as problematic as talking to boys.

"No, he doesn't," Freddie says. "He thinks you blame him for Erhart."

"He does?"

Erhart had leukemia. I don't think Daddy gave Erhart cancer.

"He doesn't think that," Mother says. "He's not stupid, though, Sophie. He's aware that you're very angry with him."

"He's just Daddy," I say. "I'm not so mad at him."

"You are too," Freddie says. "You throw that affair up in his face every chance you get."

"Okay," I say. "Trick question: How does Daddy's having an affair while Erhart is in the hospital make you a priority?"

"It had nothing to do with us," Freddie says. "Daddy was just handling everything badly."

"And Sophie has a lot of rage about how badly," Mother says. "Don't you?"

"I guess," I say.

Yes, yes, yes. I certainly have a lot of rage about how badly Daddy handled everything. But I have way more rage at myself for every botched answer on an exam and every missed opportunity to say and do the right thing. In the right way. For not always knowing what's right. For handling things badly.

"Freddie, you have to let your sister make her own peace with your father," Mother says. "Why don't you focus on telling him how you feel about the change in the holiday schedule?"

"Fine," she says. "That's just great. Thanks a lot."

And with a toss of her shiny blonde hair, she is out of the kitchen.

"Now I have a big favor to ask you," Mother says.

"Short of cleaning up my room, the answer is probably yes," I say.

Her big favor has to do with Thanksgiving, which I had guessed. And with Francis, which I had not. Francis has decided that going up to Meadowbrooke during a holiday is a bad time to see his friends. They will mostly be home visiting their families. Nick wants to show Mother the school and introduce her to his friends who live in town.

Francis wants to stay in New York. Would it be okay if Francis stayed with us? Nick doesn't want Francis to be alone during a major holiday. If he camped out with us without intruding on Daddy's visits, would that be okay?

"Sure," I say. "That would be great. It's not like we see so much of Daddy when you go out of town."

"I know," Mother says. "That's partly why your sister is so mad about the schedule switch. She was hoping that he would take you girls with him to Europe for Christmas."

"We don't see that much of him when he takes us on trips," I say.

"I know," Mother says. "So you don't mind about Francis?"

"No," I say. "Of course not. Better ask Freddie, though. I don't think she likes him."

"Interestingly enough, that is exactly what your sister said about you."

"She doesn't think I like Francis? I see Francis almost every day."

"I don't think Freddie puts a lot of faith in platonic friendships."

"You mean because we're not dating?"

"Right," Mother says. "Needless to say, if you were dating I wouldn't be arranging for him to spend the holiday here."

"Why?"

"Because I think that at a certain age, love needs to be regulated."

I picture my mother in countless hospital corridors. Sitting, waiting, hoping, and despairing. Sometimes alone. Sometimes with Daddy. I remember how at the funeral she cried in Daddy's arms as if she had never thrown him out. As if he had never given her cause. I think of how she glows on the nights she comes home from a date with Nick. I think of how I am fifteen years old and my father isn't sure if I love him or not.

"It seems to me that love always needs to be regulated," I say.

"You're probably right," Mother says. "It's just a question of who does it for whom."

In my room, I have overdue homework in math, physics, history, and Italian. Not to mention a fair amount of *Hamlet* to read. However, I push all those books aside and reach for my essay notes. I have something to add to my ramblings on *felt* and *feel*. How and why does time change not only who does the regulating, but who is loved?

SIXTEEN

The first draft of our essay is due the week before Thanksgiving. I don't have anything written except for a page and a half of questions. And all of them, when I review the list in an attempt to find even one answer, can be boiled down to one question: Why has time changed the way I think, feel, and behave? I used to think it was events that changed me. But the events — Erhart dying, Daddy's affair, my friends treating me like a girl — stay the same. I change. The way I feel about events changes.

I used to think that the leukemia killed only Erhart. But now I think that so many things died with my brother. Not just obvious stuff, like my parents' marriage, but the kind of people we all were. Freddie never cared so much about Daddy's opinion before Erhart. I wasn't so focused — so rigid. Only Mother has stayed the same, but in a few years I might think she is totally different from how I think about her now.

I try and organize all these things into five neatly typed pages. Ha! I print out draft after incoherent draft. I get up early the morning it's due because I'm doing double workouts to prepare for the swim meet next week. I look through my stack of ideas, trying to cut and paste the best version. By the time I'm done, I've missed morning practice and I have three pages covered with a cobbled-together personal exploration of time. It's not the greatest essay in the world, but it's not going to botch my English grade.

I'm doing really well in all my other classes. Mr. Kelley says that next semester, he's going to recommend that Henry and I get extra math homework. He says that geometry is too easy for us and we might as well start trying to decipher statistics.

"What's wrong with calculus?" Henry asks.

"Statistics is harder," Mr. Kelley says, and it's impossible to miss the gleam of satisfaction in his voice.

"He's a sadistic monster," Henry says.

"Just be glad we don't have extra homework in physics," I say.

Henry and I still eat lunch alone together in

the cafeteria, although both Rebecca and Justin have sat with us several times. I had to pass Rebecca a note in study hall saying that they needed to stop it. I appreciated the effort, I wrote, and the company, but Henry considered it a form of torture to have to talk to anyone other than me. Rebecca was very pleasant about it. Every time I pass one of Rebecca's A-girl friends in the hall now, they say hi. It's nice even when it's annoying.

I finally get around to showing Francis the apology Christopher wrote for Henry. I explain about uncluttered minds.

"Doesn't it bother you?" Francis asks.

"Doesn't what bother me?"

"That he never thinks about you. Henry's your best friend at school and his big desire is to never think about you."

"Why should that bother me?" I ask. "It's kind of comforting."

I know I think about Francis way too much. I'm glad Henry doesn't think about me. He's interesting, but unlike Francis, he's not demanding. I wouldn't want to be responsible for somebody wasting their thoughts on me.

Mother and Nick have planned to leave on the Monday before Thanksgiving. They're renting a car and want to beat holiday traffic. They'll drive back home on Saturday to avoid the traffic on the other end of the weekend. Mother leaves work early Monday and is home before I get back from practice. Freddie is inspecting the groceries Mother has bought to feed the three of us while she and Nick are away.

"I thought you were only going for a week," Freddie says. "There's enough food here for a month. For ten people."

"I feel nervous," Mother says. "I've never left you girls alone before just so that I could go off."

It's true. She's gone away before, but only for work. Mother's a financial consultant at a firm downtown. They participate in nationwide conferences three times a year and she has to go to those.

"You're not nervous about Nick, though, are you?" Freddie asks.

"No, not at all," Mother says.

"Good," Freddie says. "We want you to have a good time, don't we, Sophie?"

I nod. Yes, of course we do. The doorbell rings and we greet Nick and Francis, who have brought two pizzas as well as a sleeping bag.

"He wouldn't pack a suitcase," Nick says to Mother. "His clothes and toothbrush are all folded up in the sleeping bag."

Freddie goes to the kitchen for paper plates and napkins. We sit on the floor of the living room and eat pizza. Nick gives Freddie a piece of paper and an envelope.

"That's the number where you can reach us," he says. "And there's cash in the envelope for unexpected expenses."

"Nick gave me cash too," Francis says to me. "We can pay the admission price at the Met if you want."

"It will be mobbed," Freddie says. "The whole city is crawling with tourists this week."

"In a way, everyone who goes to a museum is a tourist," Francis says. "So we'll blend right in."

"Daddy says tourists are people who stay in hotels and don't know the local language," Freddie says.

"A tourist is someone who travels for plea-sure," Mother says. "So Francis is right. As long as the museum is a treat, then you are tourists while there."

Freddie puts her barely touched piece of pizza down. She covers it with her napkin. She's done. Three bites. That's her dinner.

"Where is your father taking you for Thanksgiving dinner?" Nick asks.

"Daddy doesn't really believe in Thanksgiving," I say. "He says stealing land from the Indians is nothing to celebrate."

"He likes the time off," Freddie says. "But we've never done the whole turkey thing unless we get invited by friends."

"That's terrible," Francis says.

"It's just what he thinks. He's not so wrong," I say.

"No, he's not wrong at all," Francis says. "But the meal is fun. I can cook you guys the meal."

"Really?" Freddie asks. "Pie and everything?"

"You buy the pie," Francis says. "But I can do everything else."

"There goes your unexpected-expenses money," Nick says.

"Daddy won't like it," I say. "He likes the leisure of holidays, but not the ritual."

I believe that this is a direct quote. We always celebrated Christmas, but Daddy made fun of it. "This revolting but persistent pagan festival," he would say.

"Cooking dinner will be better than the opera," Freddie says. "Daddy got tickets for us to go to the opera."

"That's way better than eating," Francis says. "I've got to say, the opera sounds cool.

What was that one you took me to where they had an elephant on stage?"

"*Aida*," Nick says.

"Which opera did your father get tickets for?" Mother ask.

"*Othello*," Freddie says. "Daddy thought that would be good for Sophie because of her English class."

"She's reading *Hamlet*," Francis says.

"He thought it was *Othello*," Freddie says.

"Do you think he ever listens to me?" I ask.

"About as much as you talk to him," Freddie says.

"Okay, time for us to go," Nick says.

I get Mother's overnight bag. She hugs Freddie. Nick hugs Francis. Then he hugs me.

"Be a good girl," he says. "Be yourself."

I hug Mother and then they're gone. Freddie and Francis change the sheets on Mother's bed. Freddie's going to sleep in there. Francis is sleeping on the floor of the living room. He says he prefers the floor to any mattress known to man. We all do homework in the kitchen. Francis is reading *Hedda Gabler*, which Freddie was supposed to have finished last month. They take turns reading it aloud while I do my physics and geometry problems. When I switch to Italian, I ask them to be quiet so I can really focus.

Instead they take the play into the living

room, but I can still hear them. Francis is having such a good time trying to talk as if he were a woman and Freddie is so obviously thrilled to have someone help with her homework. Sitting in the kitchen, I listen to their voices and think that this is what it might have been like. I know it is not very probable that Erhart and Freddie would ever have had the same reading assignment. But with Francis entertaining my sister in another part of the apartment, I can imagine — I can pretend — that we are three again.

SEVENTEEN

I have not just won, I have broken the record for fastest one-hundred-meter butterfly ever clocked at a swim meet here. Far more important is that my time was 1:02:37, which means I finally cracked 1:03. When I look up at the stands, to focus on the huge clock and check that this is really so, I see my father sitting between Henry and Francis. I must be hallucinating, since Henry never comes to school events and Daddy called last night to say he probably wouldn't make it. My chest is still heaving and my shoulders are killing me. Hallucinating is probably the inevitable result of physical pain. Coach Alden holds a towel out for me.

"Good for you, Sophie," she says, and I think of all those hours in the pool and have to agree.

We are at Trinity, a school not five blocks from Tyler Prep. Trinity is our biggest rival and this is the most important meet of the season. I haul myself out of the pool, amazed, as always, at how red and warm my skin can get in cold water. Justin hands me my sweatshirt.

"Way to go, Sophie," he says.

"Thanks," I say, wrapping the towel around my waist and pulling my sweatshirt on.

"Now you've got to do that totally over again in your leg of the relay."

I had forgotten all about the relay, and I don't know if I'll be able to lift my arms out of the water anytime soon. I hear the starter's gun go off and I slump onto the bench.

"Your dad's here," Justin says.

"I saw."

"He almost missed your whole event," Justin says. "Francis took away his cell phone."

"My father was on the phone?"

"Yup. Pretty much what mine does whenever he's around me," Justin says.

"He wasn't going to come," I say. "He must have had an attack of conscience at the last minute."

"We're up," Justin says.

He's first. I'm last. I am so tired that I don't see how I will possibly make it through another hundred meters. Fortunately, by the time my turn comes we are leading by over a length and a half. When I finish, I look back up toward my father. Henry and Francis are on their feet cheering. Daddy has one hand pressed hard against his ear and the other wrapped around the phone he is talking into. Oh, well. At least he's here.

I know that Daddy was supposed to meet Freddie at a restaurant up near Columbia, where Ian lives. Since Ian is going out of town tomorrow, Freddie wanted him to meet Daddy tonight. I don't want him running late for that on my account. Plus, I'm worried Henry and/or Francis will be waiting around downstairs for me.

Picturing the two of them trying to make small talk with my father or with each other has me dechlorinated and dressed in seven minutes flat. I take the steps two at a time with resounding thumps. Daddy is sitting on one of those orange plastic chairs that look like misshapen pears. He stands as soon as he sees me. Sometimes we hug and sometimes we very pointedly don't. It's not always up to me which one is going to happen. I see Francis and Henry standing by the water fountain in the hallway behind me, so I step out of hug's reach.

"Hi, Daddy."

"You looked just great in the water, Sophia."

And you looked really good on the phone.

"Thanks," I say. "What time are you meeting Freddie?"

"She canceled," Daddy says. "It's how I was able to come. I've got to get back to the studio. I couldn't have taken the time if I had been obliged to meet Freddie's young man."

It's always good to know that when Daddy does show up, it's for the fun of it. Not as a chore.

"Why did Freddie cancel?" I ask him.

"I don't know," he says, and with a lowered voice, "I met the son."

The son? I follow Daddy's eyes and turn around. "You mean Francis?"

"Yes," Daddy says, putting his hand to his face where the tattoo would be if it were his tear.

"He's staying with us," I say. "While Nick and Mother are away."

"So I understand."

"Well," I say. "Thanks for coming. Glad you could fit me in."

"Do you know where you girls might like to meet before the opera?"

"Freddie doesn't want to go to the opera," I say. "Francis is going to cook dinner. She'd rather we did that."

"No, she doesn't," Daddy says.

"Yes, she does." I say.

Daddy's beeper goes off. He looks at his watch.

"Call me when you decide," he says. "It was wonderful to see you."

"I could tell," I say.

He knows better than to try and hug me. He just shakes his coat out, puts it on, and leaves. I sit down on the chair he left vacant. Henry and Francis stay by the water fountain. Perhaps they are waiting to see if I explode before they approach.

"All clear," I call.

I watch them walk toward me. Henry is so small in comparison to Francis. If you didn't know, you would think Francis was the one with the black belt.

"He's a real piece of work," Francis says, looking out of the door my father has used to make his escape.

"He is who he is," I say.

"Congrats, Sophie," Henry says. "I didn't know you were that fast."

"Neither did I," I say. "What are you doing here? You never come to these things."

"I know," he says. "But I thought I should because, you know . . ."

"You thought so or Christopher did?"

"Both of us did," he says, and I am immediately relieved.

Henry is still Henry. Just like my father. Which only leaves Francis to trouble me.

"You want to come over for dinner?" I ask.

"We're having chicken with a cream sauce," Francis says. "Plus a lot of salad."

"I can't," Henry says, looking rather frightened at the prospect. "Thanks, though."

"Another time," Francis says.

"Have a happy Thanksgiving," I say.

"You too," Henry says. "Good to meet you, Francis."

Henry sounds like he really means it, and Francis smiles.

"Good meeting you too," he says, picking up my swim bag.

The three of us walk to the M104 bus which Henry takes to get home.

"He won't have much of a vacation," Francis says as we head up to Central Park West. "He's got a chess seminar in West Virginia."

"He does every year," I say. "For him, that's a holiday."

Francis says that my father didn't really like the idea of having a meal cooked for him instead of going to the opera. I tell him I knew that already and ask if he saw Freddie this afternoon before the swim meet.

"She's canceled dinner with Daddy," I say. "He was supposed to meet Ian and he says she didn't give him a reason for canceling."

"That may just mean that he didn't ask her for one," Francis says.

When we let ourselves into the apartment, I think that Freddie must be out. It's totally dark in the front hall, but there is a dull light coming from the dining room.

"She's sitting in there with just the candles lit," Francis says. "Give me your coat and go talk to her."

"Where are you going?" I ask.

"I'll hang out in your room. If she wants to talk, she won't want me around."

I reach out to grab his arm, to keep him near, to explain that Freddie and I are not so close that she will value my company. I miss his arm, however, and wind up patting at his face. Which was not what I meant and I am about to apologize, but Francis takes hold of the hand on his face and pulls me into a sort of hug. Except that it's more like a hold because I'm not really touching him.

The hand holding my wrist he's pulled behind his back and his other arm is around my back. It's so dark that I feel him more than I see him lean in towards me and then we are kissing and I have to say that it is really nice. A lot like eating marshmallows with someone who is going to live. I think he stops before I do, but maybe I pull away first. How else do you breathe when your mouth is so busy?

"I'm sorry," Francis says. "You were just unbelievably beautiful this afternoon."

If my sister weren't in the dining room sulking about God knows what, I'd clear up exactly why he's sorry every time he touches me. And I'd ask what he means by *unbelievably* and *this afternoon*. Is it so unbelievable that I might be beautiful or is it that I only was this afternoon? And why is he kissing me if he's sorry? I'd be able to figure out a lot more if I could see his face. Francis turns me around and pushes me gently toward the dining room.

"Go on," he says.

And I do. Because, frankly, my sister, with all her moods, her judgments, and her resentments, is a lot easier to understand.

EIGHTEEN

She looks a lot like I must have looked last month when Mother came home from her date and found me staring at candles. I decide to act the way Mother did. I pull out an empty chair, sit down, and say how romantic the room looks. Freddie laughs. And then she says something that takes me a second to figure out.

At first I think she's said (yet again) that Ian is a graduate student. But since there is none of the usual pride and glee shooting out of her eyes, I understand that Ian is *dating* a graduate student. He is, therefore, no longer dating Freddie.

"Oh, God," I say. "I'm so sorry. Is that why you canceled dinner with Daddy?"

"I didn't cancel dinner with Daddy," Freddie says. "Is that what he told you?"

"Yes," I say. "What happened with Ian?"

"He thinks I'm a beautiful and lovely girl,

but that he needs a deeper intellectual commitment."

"Beautiful and lovely are redundant," I say, thinking what a jerk Ian is.

Wondering again what *unbelievably beautiful* means, before shoving Francis out of my mind.

"He meant lovely like a good person," Freddie says. "I guess I wasn't smart enough for him."

"I think he wasn't smart enough," I say. "Did he ever try and do anything with you that you were interested in?"

Freddie may not be a genius at school or even interested in her homework, but she is an interesting person. She volunteers in the pediatrics ward at Mount Sinai. In college, she wants to get a degree in physical therapy so she can use massage as an emotionally healing technique for terminally ill people.

"He had no idea what I was interested in," Freddie says. "All we did was talk about him. How he felt to be working on his Ph.D. What he was studying. How hard it was for him to explain to his friends that he was dating someone in high school."

"Why?" I ask her. "Why did you only talk about him?"

I mean, it doesn't sound like she ever gave

him a chance to know her. How could he possibly tell if she was a good person, let alone an interesting one, if all they did was discuss Ian?

"You know how much easier it is to get along with Daddy if you just talk about him?" she asks, by way of an answer.

"I have noticed that," I say, rather astonished that she has.

"Well, Ian was the same way. And I knew it. I knew that he wasn't paying any more attention to me than Daddy was, but he called a lot."

"You saw him more than we saw Daddy."

"I know," Freddie says. "It's not like they were identical, but Ian was easier to be around if we did what he wanted."

"So next time you'll pick somebody who is less easy to be around," I say.

"He picked me," Freddie says. "That was the whole point of him."

"I'm really sorry," I say.

"It doesn't matter," she says. "Where's Francis?"

"Hiding in my room. He thought you might want some privacy."

"I thought I'd have a whole night of it," Freddie says. "I figured Daddy would take you guys to dinner instead."

"He had to work," I say. "He wasn't even

going to come, but when you canceled he found time."

"I did not cancel," Freddie says. "I called him to say Ian wouldn't be joining us. So he said there was no point in us going to dinner and this way he could go to your swim meet. How was it? Did you win?"

"Yes," I say. "He's such a jerk."

"He's not a jerk," Freddie says. "He only has so much time to go around."

"He talked on the phone the whole time, practically," I say. "Francis took it away during my event, but he was on it again immediately."

"Francis met Daddy? Oh my God, what did he think?"

"Daddy called him *the son.*"

"No, what did Francis think of Daddy?"

"He said he was a real piece of work," I say.

"Do you like him at all?" Freddie asks, and she sounds so sad that I know she is asking if I like our father.

Which is too bad, because I wonder more if I like Francis. It doesn't matter if I like Daddy. It won't mean anything.

"I love him," I say, fairly sure that I do.

"I love him too," Freddie says. "I wonder if he loves us, though. That makes me not like him."

"He loves you," I say. "You're the child of his heart."

"That just means he thinks you're smart."

"Do you remember what he was like before Erhart?" I ask her.

"The same as now. He was charming. He worked a lot."

"He's not that charming," I say.

"Not to you, he's not. He is to me," Freddie says. "He thinks charm irritates you. He says you're too hard to charm."

"He could try," I say, but Freddie's mind is elsewhere.

"Before Erhart I never worried about Daddy," she says. "I thought he'd always know what to do. Like, he always knew who to tip and what wine to serve at parties. How to get jobs lined up. He would be okay. Always."

I don't say anything about the doubtful value of wine selecting as a life survival skill.

"And then Erhart got sick and every chance he had, Daddy did the wrong thing."

I think of myself in the dark hallway. How I reached out to keep Francis by my side and wound up kissing him instead. How I have no idea what, if anything, that might mean. How frightening it is to love someone. How easy it might be to screw it up if the someone you love is dying.

"Maybe Daddy was scared," I say. "Before Erhart, he knew what to do because it was easy. And then it was too hard. Maybe being with us is hard now. Maybe that's why he's a jerk instead."

I am, of course, thinking of Justin Hawker, who was a jerk the minute it got hard to be around me. We, both of us, handled things quite badly. And yet, I'd say we're friends now. Which means there's hope for me and Francis. Maybe even for me and Daddy.

"I thought you were mad at him," Freddie says. "Where's all that rage Mother says you have?"

"I am mad at him," I say. "But ever since Erhart, you and I have been different. Maybe Daddy is different, too, and we don't like him for that."

"The only difference is, now I sometimes wonder if he loves us. Before Erhart, I never did."

I do a brief calculation in my head. Since my father moved out (was thrown out, whatever you want to call it) I have gone out with him and Freddie at least forty-two times. And yet I have never once suspected that my sister thought Daddy was anything less than perfect. It just goes to show how hard it is to know what people feel if they don't tell you.

"You didn't give him a chance tonight, Freddie. You should have told him about you and Ian. He would have made time for you."

"Sure," she says. "But he would have had to skip your swim meet."

"That would have been fine," I say. "Believe me."

"I want to be part of his schedule," she says. "I'm tired of trying to fit into it."

"You should tell him that," I say.

"Where?" she asks. "At the opera? I am not going to the damn opera."

"Call him at the studio right now," I say. "It's a half day of school tomorrow. Daddy could maybe take you out to a late dinner and you can tell him that you're not going to the opera and that he should make you more of a priority."

"Just like that?" Freddie asks. "Can't you make it sound more pretty?"

"It is pretty," I say. "You love him and you want him to love you back and you're not dying. He has to deal with you."

"Doesn't he have to deal with you too?"

"I have to let him," I say. "I'm a little behind you in this area."

She considers this. Stands up and blows the candles out. I turn the light on and we sit back down. She looks so pretty even though her eyes

are kind of puffy. I hope that with Daddy she
will be more focused on herself than she was
with Ian. I hope my father will treat her well.
No matter how hard it is.

NINETEEN

Daddy tells Freddie to come down to the studio. He'll buy her a drink and they can have a good talk.

"He knows you're not twenty-one yet, right?" Francis asks.

"He didn't mean a real drink," Freddie says. "He meant, like, it will be nine o'clock before he's free. Kind of late for supper and too early for a midnight dinner."

"When are you going to eat?" Francis asks.

"I'm not that hungry," she says.

"What about you?" Francis asks me.

"I could eat," I say.

I have decided that if Francis can act like nothing happened in the hallway, so can I. Saying I am so tense that the thought of eating makes me want to throw up is, therefore, out of the question.

"I'll make you a salad," Francis says to Freddie. "Dressing on the side. Sophie and I will eat real food."

At around eight-thirty, Francis goes downstairs to hail a cab for my sister. It's not like we both haven't been standing in the middle of the street waving down taxis since forever, but Freddie likes the idea of Francis doing this well-practiced maneuver for her. I go into my bedroom to have an on-purpose memory of Erhart. Only nothing comes to mind. Not even the images. I can't even bring up the bad ones. Like the time his IV tore loose and there was blood and medicine all over the top sheet in his last hospital bed. I know for a fact it happened, but I can't picture it. Although, I was there. Mother was in the hallway talking to a doctor.

Why can't I see it? Or feel what it was like to watch the blood spread and not know what to do? Where is the panic I felt that afternoon? I look up at the ceiling hook. Surely that will get me started. Nothing. I might as well hang a plant from it, if this is all the help it's going to give me. Great. I'm a good swimmer, but a wretched daughter, a nonexistent girlfriend, and a sister who can't remember one tiny thing about her brother.

"Sophie?"

It's Francis, standing half hidden behind my door.

"I knocked," he says.

I can't say anything. I start to open my mouth, but the lump in my throat alerts me to the fact that my eyes are burning and blurring.

"You're crying," he says, stepping out from behind the door and walking into the room.

"Don't," I say. "Don't touch me. You'll just be sorry."

Francis kneels down next to my chair.

"What are you talking about?"

"Like in the hallway," I say, relieved that being angry at him has made it possible to talk and cry at the same time. "You were sorry."

"What, you mean, tonight? Sophie, I kissed you."

"I know," I say. "I was there."

"I thought you were mad. You jerked away like I had bitten you or something."

"I was trying to breathe," I say.

"Well, you've made it really clear that I can't do that," Francis says.

"What, breathe? I don't mind if you breathe."

"No," he says. "Kiss you. I know that's not the kind of friends you want to be. And I've really worked to respect that. That's why I was sorry."

"Oh," I say. "I thought you were sorry because I wasn't an A-girl."

"No. A-girls are boring."

"Rebecca's nice," I say.

"Nice can be boring," Francis says. "You didn't mind the kiss?"

He looks totally confused. And thrilled. Francis looks thrilled at the idea that I might have liked kissing him.

"It was really nice," I say.

He smiles. I realize that I have almost called his kissing me boring.

"So *not* boring," I say quickly. "I thought you would never do that."

"I thought you never wanted me to and then when you touched me it just slipped out."

"What did?" I ask, wanting to hear him say it.

That I am believably beautiful. To him. Francis puts his hand on my knee. I look at him for a second, mentally listing a few things I know about geometry, physics, and Italian before covering his hand with my own. He stands up and pulls me with him. My hands are shaking again, but I notice his are, too.

He whispers, "Breathe through your nose."

And then he kisses me. In my brightly lit bedroom. Still very nice. But totally different from eating marshmallows with someone who is going to live. When we are done kissing, I look up at the ceiling and I know with every part of my body how empty things are without Erhart. I have five accidental memories in a row of my brother. I lean against Francis, who has wrapped his arms around me. Funny that I am full of memories about Erhart at the exact same time that I am full of happiness about Francis. When did time become so wide? So very generous?

Francis asks if I still want to go to medical school. When I say yes, he sits down on the floor, leaning against the bed.

"So we could actually date without cluttering your mind," he says.

I take hold of his hand. I feel exactly like myself, only a little happier than usual.

"Yes," I say. "How about your mind?"

"Mine was cluttered from not dating," he says.

"Oh," I say. "You disguised that really well."

"I am an expert at hiding what I think."

"Good," I say. "We need to not tell Nick or my mother."

"I tell Nick everything," Francis says. "And

he really likes you. So it will be happy news to him."

I repeat what Mother told me about love needing to be regulated, only I don't use the word *love*. After all, I have no idea if that is what's going on here. There's a line between friends and dating so I expect there's another one between dating and love.

"Oh, sure," Francis says. "They'll never leave us alone in an apartment again. At least not overnight."

"What if they want to move in together?" I ask. "Or get married? I don't want to complicate things for them."

"Jeez, Sophie, don't borrow trouble," he says. "What if they break up? What if you meet somebody else? What if I get hit by a truck tomorrow?"

"I'm not going to meet anyone else," I say. "And be careful when you cross the street."

Francis laughs. "What I'm trying to say is that if Nick and your mother want to get married when you and I are still in need of 'regulation' then they'll find a way to work around it."

Spoken like someone who has no idea of where he wants to go to college and even less of a clue of what he wants to do afterwards. I probably like Francis for not being as much of a plan-ahead type as I am, but the reality is that horrible things happen and it's better to be prepared.

"There are some things we can plan," Francis says. "The kind of obvious stuff that comes up when you're dating."

"What kind of stuff?"

As far as I can tell there is nothing obvious about dating.

"You know, the kind of stuff your mother wants to regulate."

Oh, no. He totally means sex. I'm so not prepared for sex.

"That will be a while," I say.

"Yeah, I figure. But it should be something that we discuss instead of letting it divide us."

"Is that what happened with you and Alicia?"

"The problem with Alicia was that there was never anything else to do. She never wanted to go anywhere, and talking to her made me miserable."

"You broke up with Alicia because all you could do with her was have sex?"

"She broke up with me because she thought so," Francis says. "For the record, I would have been happy to do other things. She wasn't interested in a lot."

Since I am interested in almost everything, I

figure I can put off having sex with Francis until
. . . I want to. I sit down on the floor next to him
and we spend the three hours while Freddie is
gone kissing. And — not my suggestion — reading *Hamlet* aloud. Turns out that Francis likes
the sword fighting as much as Henry does. His
favorite part is when Hamlet decides to not kill
his uncle while he is praying. Francis says it is
the best example of Hamlet being able to talk
himself out of any and all positive actions.

Note to self: I like kissing better than doing
homework. Who knew?

TWENTY

Thanksgiving day passes rather pleasantly. Daddy works out a compromise with Freddie about what to do. He takes Francis and me to see *Othello* and then comes back to the apartment to eat the meal which Francis started before we left and which Freddie has finished putting together. Daddy is very charming. Not to me, I notice, but in being so funny and interested in Freddie and Francis, I know he is making an effort on my behalf.

Daddy apparently told Freddie that when a man says he needs a "deeper intellectual commitment," he thinks he's not smart enough for the woman he's breaking up with. While I doubt that this is true, I'm glad Daddy came up with something to make my sister feel better. He and Francis have an endless discussion about the history of tattoos in different cultures. They spend at least half an hour debating henna. Daddy thinks that the intricate patterns Indian women paint on their skin is the same as getting a tattoo. Francis says that the level of permanence is what makes a tattoo special.

When Daddy leaves, we do the dishes. I load the washer, Francis tackles the pots, and Freddie does all the fragile china. Daddy told us he'd be up for anything we suggested doing tomorrow. He's flying to California on Saturday. He's got a meeting there on Monday, but like Mother and Nick, he is traveling early so as to avoid the holiday traffic.

Freddie wants to see a movie and I'd like to go to the museum. There are things about Daddy I miss and listening to him go on and on about art is one of them. He never says anything that I can understand, but I like how totally dedicated he is to the topic. Daddy in a museum is like focus personified.

"Why don't you go with your father to visit Erhart?" Francis asks, interrupting the argument Freddie and I are having about what would be more fun.

Freddie and I look at each other.

"Erhart's dead," Freddie says.

"Exactly," Francis says.

"Exactly what?" Freddie asks, her tone reminiscent of the one she used when she asked him why he called his father Nick.

"It's just that you can go to a museum or a

movie anytime," Francis says.

"Not in Daddy's company," I say.

"All the more reason you should use his company for something not so ordinary," he says. "Like visiting Erhart."

"How do you suggest we do that?" Freddie asks.

"When my mother died, Nick and I used to spend part of every holiday visiting her."

"You mean in a cemetery?" Freddie asks.

"No. She was cremated and we spread her ashes in my grandmother's backyard."

"Erhart was buried," I say.

"In a cemetery uptown," Freddie says.

It's called Trinity Cemetery, and it's on 155th Street between Broadway and Riverside. It's not the greatest neighborhood, but Trinity Church, downtown on Wall Street, ran out of room to bury people and I guess they got land where they could.

"We've never been there," Freddie says.

"Are you serious?" Francis asks. "Nick took me to where her ashes were every holiday for five years."

"They thought we were too young," I say, although I once heard Mother tell someone that Daddy couldn't bear the idea of watching his daughters bury his son.

"They thought *she* was too young," Freddie says.

I decide that Freddie doesn't need to know what he really thought.

"That's not right," Francis says. "Sophie, I'm surprised you let them do that to you."

"You only went for five years?" Freddie asks him. "To where her ashes are?"

"We moved," Francis says. "And also, after a while we got used to her being gone. We didn't need to do anything special to include her in our holiday. Her being dead is part of who we are."

"Remembering Erhart is part of who I am," Freddie says. "His dying will never be part of me."

I never thought I'd see the day when my sister explains how I feel.

"Still and all, he is dead," Francis says. "You owe it to yourselves to see where he's buried. Not ever going is inexcusable."

"Daddy will never want to do that," I say. "So I guess it's a movie. At least he can't use his phone in one."

"We should at least ask," Freddie says. "He might like to . . . see Erhart. He always says Mother gets to do all the remembering because she lives with us."

"Ask him then," I say, wondering if it will

ever occur to her that Mother gets to do all the remembering because she makes time for us.

"No," Freddie says. "You ask him. I don't like to bring Erhart up with him."

"Why?" Francis asks.

"I don't like to upset him," she says. "But Sophie doesn't mind."

"I do mind upsetting him," I say.

I also mind being upset *by* him. Does she think she's the only person Daddy has driven into the dining room with the lights off and the candles lit?

"So you guys never discuss Erhart around you father?"

"Rarely," I say.

"There was so much going on when he died," Freddie says. "It was just horrible. What's to discuss?"

"You could talk about the parts of your brother's life that don't have to do with his dying."

"You'd think so," Freddie says. "The problem is he got sick when he was only six and he died less than two years later."

"You have to work to think about him and not think about the dying," I say.

"Yeah, I remember that," Francis says, touching the tattoo on his face.

I don't think he has any idea how often he

touches it when he's talking about his mother.

"I was eight when my mother died and for a really long time it seemed like my strongest memory of her was the dying part."

"Then what happened?" Freddie asks.

"I don't know," he says. "Maybe once I got used to her being dead, it stopped being such a big deal."

"Can you think about her now without thinking about her being dead?" I ask.

"No," he says, touching his face. "Her death is a part of her life. And of mine."

A long silence creeps up on us. I can't speak for Freddie, but I am thinking Francis has a point. I am doing Erhart's memory no favors by only calling it to mind twice a day. It's not accidental memories which are disrespectful so much as edited ones. Erhart died when he was very young. I'd say that was the defining event of his life. It's ridiculous of me to remember him without including that fact.

"Will you come with us?" Freddie asks. "To where Erhart is buried?"

"Sure," Francis says. "If it's okay with your father."

"It's not just up to him," she says. "You ask him, though, okay, Sophie?"

"No," I say. "You ask him."

"I'll ask him," Francis says.

"That's too pathetic," I say. "I'll do it."

I make them leave the room. If I'm going to sound at all, in my mother's words, "normal and healthy weaving Erhart into conversation" with my father, I can't have an audience. Turns out to be an incredibly easy discussion. Daddy says he goes up to the cemetery once a week. After being out of town, the first thing he does is visit Erhart's grave.

"Why?"

"It's how I remember," Daddy says. "You'd be appalled at how much I forget about him on a daily basis."

"No," I say. "Probably not."

"It took months for me to realize that my memories were going to shift around as I got further and further away from his death," Daddy says. "Going to the cemetery is like a way of checking in with him."

I ask if Francis can come. Daddy says of course and asks if he should get his car out of the garage.

"We can use the subway," I say, knowing how he hates to put his car (a powder blue Lexus he got for himself the year he turned forty) at risk for scratches or break-ins.

"The car will be more pleasant," he says.

"Okay."

He tells me to sleep well and hangs up just in time for me to tell the dial tone I love it. And then, since I have its complete and undivided attention, I add that I don't think it gave Erhart cancer. I make no mention of the affair or of his job for love. Time will need to get a little wider, a tad more generous, before I can love Daddy while thinking about those things.

TWENTY-ONE

I t's in the car, the much-beloved, well-cared-for and pristine car, that I finally accomplish what my body has been threatening to do for over two years: throw up. Freddie is in the front with Daddy. She is fiddling with the CD player. Francis and I are in the back, watching the streets change from clean to shabby to wrecked. Daddy is saying how nice this is for him. How comforting to be on his way to this place with company.

"I brought Julia here a couple of times," he says. "But nothing replaces family."

Julia is the name of the woman Daddy had the affair with. When Erhart was still alive and Daddy was still living at home. If he really believes nothing replaces family, he might have thought twice before sleeping with Julia. Let alone taking her to see Erhart.

"You took Julia to the cemetery?" Freddie asks.

"Certainly," Daddy says. "Is that a problem?"

"No," Freddie says. "I was just asking."

Oh, no. Of course not. We don't get to be there when Erhart is buried because Daddy doesn't want to see his daughters bury his son. But he gets to bring his girlfriend because, in the end, this is all about him.

"You need to stop the car," I say, pulling at the door handle.

The Lexus has a power-lock system. I'm going to throw up all over my father's leather and carpeted clean car.

"What's wrong?" Francis asks.

"Why should I stop the car?" Daddy asks.

"She's going to be sick," Francis says as I vomit up into my mouth. "Pull over."

Daddy unlocks the car using a switch on his steering wheel and pulls over at a bus stop. I lean over, open my mouth, and throw up onto the street. A little bit gets on my knees. Francis, who is patting my back, hands me some Kleenex.

"Sssshhhh," he says. "It's okay."

Freddie gets out of the car and comes around to my side.

"Good thing you skipped breakfast," she says.

"Is she done?" I hear Daddy ask Francis.

I am with you, you stupid, thoughtless idiot.

"Yes," I say, wiping my mouth and my jean-covered knees. "Yes."

Freddie takes the tissues and tosses them in a plastic trash bin at the corner.

"He doesn't know any better," she says softly to me before getting back in the car.

She has me scoot over so that the three of us are in the back.

"I feel like a chauffeur," Daddy says.

"There are worse things," I say.

Like taking your girlfriend to your son's graveyard. I don't say this, although I do wonder: Is throwing up really such an improvement on speaking my mind? As we head further uptown, the store awnings and window signs are all in Spanish. We pass a whole block of high gray walls before Daddy turns left onto 155th Street and parks across from a narrow entrance.

Once inside the walls, we pass several fenced-off garden areas where there are clusters of tombstones instead of flower beds. There is an inscription on the back of one which catches my eye: WHAT WE LOVE, WE ARE. Right next to it, on the back of another tombstone, it says, NOT CHANGED, BUT GLORIFIED. Now what does that mean? And who was clever enough to think of, "What we love, we are"? And is it true? Does that make me Mother and Freddie and Francis and Erhart? I'll have to come back this way and give the area closer inspection.

We follow Daddy down the main path. Immediately on our right are five huge stone squares with plaques on them. Mausoleums. The first one has lots of little compartments. This is where people who are cremated get put. What is the point of being set on fire if you're not going to be spread around, but sealed up in stone? The second two squares form what is called the Court of Grace. In each square there's ten rows of twenty coffin spaces. You can see people's names carved into the separate spaces, along with their birth and death dates.

"Doesn't Erhart have a tombstone? Like in the ground?" Freddie asks, as we walk in between the last two squares, which form the Court of Hope.

"There was no room," Daddy says. "The cemetery built the mausoleums because there's no more room in the ground."

He puts his hand on a space, which is fifth in the third row from the bottom. I count before I look.

Erhart Aldrich Merdinger, May 11, 1984 – May 6, 1992.

There's a little gold cross between his name and the dates.

"I'd forgotten about the Aldrich," I say.

"Me too," Freddie says. "How could we have forgotten that?"

"It's your Mother's maiden name," Daddy says. "He was her first son as well as mine, and we felt that her family should be in his name as well."

"That's not what I meant," Freddie says.

"We know where the Aldrich is from," I tell him. "Why is there a cross?"

I notice that Erhart's is the only square that has one.

"I was raised Catholic," Daddy says.

"But you don't believe in God," I say. "You don't even approve of Christmas."

"I am indeed a doubter," Daddy says. "But it seemed important to put a cross on my son's grave."

"As long as it was important to you," I say.

Francis takes my hand.

"Look," he says. "Erhart has all this company."

Freddie and I examine the names on the other squares, which Francis is pointing to: THOMAS COLE, 1917-1992; ALFRED BAILEY, 1905-1980; ESPERANZA P. MEDINA, R.N. 1936-1991.

"I'm glad there's a nurse," Freddie says. "Erhart liked all of his."

I ask if I can go and look at other tombstones.

"Of course," Daddy says.

Freddie is running her fingers over the cross on Erhart's square. Over and over. As if the cross is a pressure point on our brother's grave and Freddie is giving it a massage. I say that I'll be right back and head for the tombstone I saw coming in.

It's a Juliet Kemp Tyron who has WHAT WE LOVE, WE ARE on the back of her tombstone, and a George Kemp who was "not changed, but glorified." You can tell by the dates that George died well before Juliet, so that "Tyron" is probably from her second marriage. I might wonder why she didn't get buried with her second husband, but a little tombstone standing in front of hers and George's explains.

DOUGLAS, DEARLY BELOVED CHILD OF GEORGE AND JULIET KEMP. BORN NOVEMBER 17, 1880. DIED DECEMBER 5, 1884.

Four! Erhart lived almost twice as long as dearly beloved Douglas did. I sit down next to this little stone. I wonder if I'm going to have to cry or throw up again, but I feel oddly happy here with Douglas and both of his parents. I had never thought before how it might be a good thing that Erhart stays the same no matter how much time moves me around. George and Juliet didn't end their lives together, but by never moving from this spot, their dearly beloved four-year-old Douglas kept them linked.

My father might bring a hundred more women here to visit Erhart. I might never understand why his reaction to Erhart's illness was to get another job which required an endless amount of travel. I might become a doctor. Or not. Nick and Mother might get married. I might be with Francis for the rest of my life or we could drift apart when and if he goes to college. I will never crack time's secrets save for one: My brother is now dead and will be for eternity.

That secret is central to who I am and to who my father is. If that's all we have to link us, it's still a lot. I hear someone walk up behind me. I know it's Francis because it would never occur to my father to search me out and it will be a while before Freddie can leave Erhart's space in the Court of Hope.

"I was thinking of your mother," I say.

Francis puts out a hand and I lace my fingers through his.

"I didn't want to interrupt," he says. "I thought you were having an on-purpose memory."

We both look down at Juliet Kemp Tyron's tombstone.

"I don't do those anymore," I say. "I am an on-purpose memory."

"Yes," he says. "I've always thought so."

On the main path, my father and Freddie are walking slowly past. If I am what I love, there I go. With part of me buried forever, but enough left over to be with Mother in Massachusetts. Not to mention spread through my dreams of Italian *caffès,* research laboratories, and the perfect English essay.

I give Francis's hand a little squeeze and know that in this instant, be it a line or a circle, generous or narrow, here I am.